THE **DADDY** CLUB

P9-EDH-472

Single fathers have it rough!
So holds the philosophy of The Daddy Club.

The club is run by men, for men.
The focus: raising children.

A veteran club member will be able to change
a diaper in record time, give a bath without
drowning the child or himself and make a grilled
cheese sandwich a gourmet chef would envy.

It's not rocket science, though that might be easier.
It's just about being the best dad a man can be.

Meetings held at Ruth Naomi's Hardware and
Muffin Shop alternate Wednesdays, 8:00 p.m.

Please join us!

This month:
HAR #813 FOUR REASONS FOR FATHERHOOD
by Muriel Jensen

Also available:
HAR #805 FAMILY TO BE by Linda Cajio

HAR #809 A PREGNANCY AND A PROPOSAL
by Mindy Neff

Dear Reader,

February is a month made for romance, and here at Harlequin American Romance we invite *you* to be our Valentine!

Every month, we bring you four reasons to celebrate romance, and beloved author Muriel Jensen has reasons of her own—*Four Reasons for Fatherhood,* to be precise. Join former workaholic Aaron Bradley as he learns about parenthood—and love—from four feisty youngsters and one determined lady in the finale to our exciting miniseries THE DADDY CLUB.

Some men just have a way with women, and our next two heroes are no exception. In Pamela Bauer's *Corporate Cowboy,* when Austin Bennett hits his head and loses his memory, Kacy Judd better watch out—because her formerly arrogant boss is suddenly the most irresistible man in town! And in *Married by Midnight* by Mollie Molay, Maxwell Taylor has more charm than even he suspects—he goes to a wedding one day, and wakes up married the next!

And if you're wondering HOW TO MARRY... *The World's Best Dad,* look no farther than Valerie Taylor's heartwarming tale. Julie Miles may not follow her own advice, but she's got gorgeous Ben Harbison's attention anyway!

We hope you enjoy every romantic minute of our four wonderful stories.

Warm wishes,

Melissa Jeglinski
Associate Senior Editor

Four Reasons for Fatherhood

MURIEL JENSEN

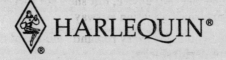

HARLEQUIN®

TORONTO • NEW YORK • LONDON
AMSTERDAM • PARIS • SYDNEY • HAMBURG
STOCKHOLM • ATHENS • TOKYO • MILAN • MADRID
PRAGUE • WARSAW • BUDAPEST • AUCKLAND

To Jeannette and Manny Braga—our best buddies!

ISBN 0-373-16813-6

FOUR REASONS FOR FATHERHOOD

Copyright © 2000 by Muriel Jensen.

Visit us at www.romance.net

Printed in U.S.A.

ABOUT THE AUTHOR

Muriel Jensen and her husband, Ron, live in Astoria, Oregon, in an old four-square Victorian at the mouth of the Columbia River. They share their home with a golden retriever/golden Labrador mix named Amber, and five cats who moved in with them without an invitation. (Muriel insists that a plate of Friskies and a bowl of water are *not* an invitation!)

They also have three children and their families in their lives—a veritable crowd of the most interesting people and children. They also have irreplaceable friends, wonderful neighbors and "a life they know they don't deserve but love desperately anyway."

Books by Muriel Jensen

HARLEQUIN AMERICAN ROMANCE

119—LOVERS NEVER LOSE
176—THE MALLORY TOUCH
200—FANTASIES & MEMORIES
219—LOVE AND LAVENDER
244—THE DUCK SHACK AGREEMENT
267—STRINGS
283—SIDE BY SIDE
321—A CAROL CHRISTMAS
339—EVERYTHING
392—THE MIRACLE
414—RACING WITH THE MOON
425—VALENTINE HEARTS AND FLOWERS
464—MIDDLE OF THE RAINBOW
478—ONE AND ONE MAKES THREE
507—THE UNEXPECTED GROOM
522—NIGHT PRINCE
534—MAKE-BELIEVE MOM
549—THE WEDDING GAMBLE
569—THE COURTSHIP OF DUSTY'S DADDY
603—MOMMY ON BOARD
606—MAKE WAY FOR MOMMY
610—MERRY CHRISTMAS, MOMMY!
654—THE COMEBACK MOM
669—THE PRINCE, THE LADY & THE TOWER
688—KIDS & CO.
705—CHRISTMAS IN THE COUNTRY
737—DADDY BY DEFAULT
742—DADDY BY DESIGN
746—DADDY BY DESTINY
756—GIFT-WRAPPED DAD
798—COUNTDOWN TO BABY
813—FOUR REASONS FOR FATHERHOOD

Don't miss any of our special offers. Write to us at the following address for information on our newest releases.

Harlequin Reader Service
U.S.: 3010 Walden Ave., P.O. Box 1325, Buffalo, NY 14269
Canadian: P.O. Box 609, Fort Erie, Ont. L2A 5X3

Upcoming topics

Week 1:	Too much Testosterone! Tales from a father of four sons
Week 2:	Peanut Butter Is Your Friend 25 creative school lunches your kid will eat
Week 3:	Fire and Hire AND Punt, Pass and Kick 'Cause you're a businessman by day but a dad *all* day
Week 4:	"Dad, did we lose electricity?" How to seduce that special someone...'cause dads need love, too!

Be there...
for information vital to every single father!

Chapter One

Susan Turner watched the long silver limo pull up in front of the church as she walked down the steps carrying Ringo, the other three boys trailing behind her. The back door on the passenger side opened before the driver could come around to help.

A tall man in a beige raincoat stepped out onto the sidewalk. He frowned apparently at the sight of the small crowd leaving the church.

"Uncle Aaron!" John shouted. They were the first words except for "yes" or "no" the boy had spoken since Susan had sped across Princeton to care for him and his brothers.

The man opened his arms and bent down to scoop up the boy as he flew at him.

"Who's that?" George asked. He was four.

"I Guess it's Uncle Aaron," six-year-old Paul replied sagely. "Come on!"

The two boys ran to the man. He lowered John to his feet to embrace the other two boys.

Susan tried not to be offended by their traitorous behaviour. She'd run to be with them the moment she'd received the news that their mother, Susan's cousin, and their father had perished in a commuter-plane crash off Catalina Island.

Ringo, the fifteen-month-old in her arms, was grateful to be held, a source of security within the chaos his little life had become. George was warm and sweet, and Paul seemed to observe and analyze everything. But though the boys knew her well, they resisted her efforts to help them with their grief, because John, almost eight, the eldest and therefore the leader, was keeping his distance, unwilling to let anyone try to take his parents' places.

Susan watched the man, who was down on one knee on the sidewalk drawing the boys into the circle of his arms as they talked. His hair was dark blond and a little rumpled from the blustery late March weather.

Hazel eyes focused on one boy after the other as he spoke earnestly to them. George on his raised knee, Paul leaning against him on one side and John on the other.

So, this was Dave's brother, Susan thought. She'd never met him, but Becky had told her about her clever in-law with the multi-million-dollar computer-software company. "He's a great guy, but when he's working he's all business, and when he's playing he's the quintessential playboy. He visits at Christmas every four or five years and calls occasionally, but he has very little time for domesticity." Then Becky had smiled; Susan had been visiting shortly after John was born. "That's why Dave and I would like to name you in our will as John's guardian should—God forbid—anything happen to us."

Susan had agreed without even stopping to consider, certain that nothing could happen to the robust young woman of twenty-one and her twenty-four-year-old husband.

But apparently God hadn't forbidden, and eight years and three more children later, Susan was having to live up to her promise.

She was more than willing. Becky had been her childhood companion, and, after their parents had passed away, her only tie to family.

She couldn't help, though, feeling resentful of the boys' business-mogul/playboy uncle, who hadn't bothered to get in touch until last night, four days after the accident. Who hadn't even made it to New Jersey on time for his brother and sister-in-law's memorial service today. And who now had the boys mesmerized like some London Fog-clad Svengali.

Then he got to his feet and bringing the boys with him, met Susan at the bottom of the steps.

He took Ringo from her and hugged him. The toddler allowed it, though he studied him a little warily.

"Hey, pal," the man said, "I'm your uncle Aaron. I'm glad to see you got the Bradley good looks, too." He pinched Ringo's nose between his knuckles and the boy giggled.

Aaron Bradley's gaze moved to Susan and rested on her a moment before he spoke, as though he thought he might analyze and understand her first.

It surprised her when she saw the slight shift in his eyes from open friendliness to cautious reserve. Had he been able to read her resentment?

He held Ringo in one arm and offered her his free hand. "You must be Susan," he said closing his hand over hers. It was large and warm. "We spoke last night on the phone. I'm Aaron Bradley, Dave's brother."

She smiled politely. "Yes, I know," she said. "I'm so sorry for your loss."

"Thank you. I'm sorry for yours." He withdrew his hand and angled his chin toward the church. "I can't believe I missed the memorial service."

"Crisis at the office?" she asked. The question had been a little glib, and she saw in his eyes that he'd noted that.

"Fog in San Francisco, actually," he replied after a moment, his voice quiet and controlled. "My connecting flight got socked in for a couple of hours."

"Aaron," a male voice called from behind Susan. "Hi. I'm sorry about Dave."

Aaron's grim features brightened into a smile as he extended his hand again. "Micah! How are you?"

A big dark-haired man in a cashmere coat came around Susan to shake hands with Aaron Bradley. "I'm good," he said. "I was hoping I'd get a chance to see you, but when you weren't in church, I was afraid something prevented you from coming."

"I was just telling Susan that my flight was delayed by fog in San Francisco. Susan, I'd like you to meet Micah Steadwell, an old school friend of mine. Micah, this is Susan Turner, Dave's wife's cousin."

Micah took her hand and brought it to his lips to plant a kiss on her knuckles. His courtly behavior was a surprise, but didn't seem like an act. He was a man, she guessed, with a unique style.

"Hello Ms. Turner," he said gravely. "I'm so sorry about your cousin."

"Thank you, Mr. Steadwell," she replied.

Micah turned to Aaron. "Are you taking the boys home with you?"

Aaron indicated Susan with a jut of his chin. "No, Dave and Becky wanted Susan to have custody."

Micah nodded. "Of course. Well." He clapped Aaron on the shoulder. "I own the Knight Club now, near the Princeton Shopping Center. I'd like you and Susan to come as my guests before you go home. I know you don't feel like partying, but I'd love to treat you to dinner if you have time."

Aaron shook his head apologetically. "Doesn't look good. I'll only be here a couple of days. But I appreciate that you came, Micah."

"Sure." Micah shook his hand again and handed him a business card. "We'll have to stay in better touch. Mom and Ross said to say hello."

Aaron nodded. "Give them my love."

"Will do. Bye, Ms. Turner."

As Micah left Aaron pointed behind him to the limousine, the liveried driver waiting by the rear passenger door. "Susan, let me take you and the boys home."

She pointed to a man and woman standing off to one side, waiting. "Those are friends of Dave's and Becky's who drove us to the church. They're waiting to—"

He handed Ringo back to her. "You get the boys into the limo and I'll explain."

He had covered the few steps to the waiting couple and was already smiling and shaking hands before she could protest. As large drops of rain began to fall, accompanied by a low rumble of thunder, she herded the other three boys toward the limo with her free hand.

The driver, a rotund older man with a cheerful expression, opened the door for them and held Ringo for her while she climbed inside. Then he handed the toddler in.

The boys were immediately pushing buttons opening and closing windows and the privacy panel, turning on the small television, discovering the wine decanter and glasses.

Since she'd arrived in their home, Susan had learned that a mother of four boys should be equipped with eight arms.

She was still trying to reclaim control when Aaron climbed into the limo and sat opposite her. He took the crystal stopper from Paul, replaced it in the decanter, closed the windows, turned off the overhead light, then found cartoons on the television.

The boys were instantly glued to it. Susan scrambled around to buckle seat belts. Aaron glanced at his watch. "Nearly noon," he said. "Should we go to lunch?"

"Uh..." She had an instant image of the ordeal mealtime had been during the past few days. John ate nothing, Paul ate everything, George made designs with his food, and Ringo preferred to see his food on the floor. And while all this was going on, the boys harrassed each other mercilessly. "I'm not sure that's a good idea. Socially, I mean."

"We'll go to a fast-food place," he countered, "where they're used to dealing with messy kids. And the kids might enjoy the playland thing, get to blow off some steam."

That was true. "All right." She glanced at his expensive raincoat. "But you might want to cover yourself in plastic. There's food over everything when they're finished eating."

He shrugged off the warning. "Winston," he called through the open privacy screen, "Find us a Burger Hut."

"You got it, Mr. Bradley."

The boys made a pretext of eating, but once they spotted the maze of wide plastic tubes through which other children chased each other, food was secondary to the desire to join them. Ringo, mercifully, had fallen asleep in Susan's lap.

"Can we go now, Uncle Aaron?" John pleaded. The other two boys jumped up and down in anticipation.

Aaron deferred to Susan. It was a diplomatic gesture she could appreciate in sentiment, but considering the boys seemed suddenly to revolve in his orbit, it was an empty concession.

But she would have to deal with them when he was gone, so she took control. "Yes, you can, but no punching or kicking or you'll have to come in. I'll be able to watch you through the window."

They nodded in unison, pushing and shoving each other before they even got to the door that led to the covered play area.

AARON STUDIED the young woman across the table from him as she shifted the child from the crook of her arm to lean against her breast. Where her silky black blouse plunged into a V neck, her skin was alabaster in contrast. Her eyes were dark and soft, with shadowy patches under them as though she was very tired. Her cheeks were pink, her lips the color of Chianti, and the whole berries-and-cream look of her was set off by thick dark hair that was caught back in a knot.

She didn't like him. He'd sensed that the moment he stepped up to her at the church. He smiled privately at the realization that Dave and Becky had probably told her that he didn't visit often enough, didn't keep in close enough touch.

"When I expressed concern for the children last night on the phone," he said without preamble, "you told me that Dave and Becky's will makes you the children's guardian."

She met his eyes directly. "That's right. I hope that doesn't offend you."

He suspected she added that as a concession to good manners.

He shook his head. "Not at all. I wish I was equipped to care for four children, but I'm really not. I travel a lot, I work long hours..." He laughed. "And my housekeeper swears."

"A man?" she asked.

"No, a woman. Heart of gold, but a strong opinionated lady. Beebee likes to think she runs my life. And the lives of whoever comes in contact with me. Anyway, I know how much my brother loved his family. If he and Becky put the boys in your care, I know you have to be a model of motherhood."

She made a scornful sound. "Hardly. But I have a house and a steady job and I made a promise to Becky."

"What do you do?"

"I'm a carpenter," she replied.

He was sure he'd misheard her. "A carpenter. Like on a construction site?"

"Not anymore." Ringo stirred and she patted his back until he resettled himself, his lips open in an oval like a little fish's mouth. "Now I have a weekly-TV cable show for women on how to use tools, do small repairs, simplify difficult or heavy jobs. I'm sponsored by Legacy Tools on the Crafters' Channel."

He found that fascinating. He wasn't much of a handyman himself. "Well, good for you. But that must take a lot of time. What'll you do about the boys? Can you afford to hire help?"

She raised an eyebrow, her expression at once indignant and imperious. She opened her mouth to reply but he cut her off before she could.

"I wasn't questioning your household management or your ability to care for them. I was just wondering if there was something I could do to help."

"Thank you," she said, "but I understand you're pretty busy with your business and your…your…"

He might have helped her had he known what she was trying to say. Since he didn't, he simply waited.

"Your…life-style," she finally finished with a slightly aggressive tilt to her chin.

"My life-style," he repeated trying to remember when he'd last had time to have one.

"You know," she said looking a little uncomfortable, though she seemed determined to ignore such a feeling as she went on intrepidly, "Your parties. Your women. Your nude sunbathing with Mariah Havilland."

He laughed. "Now, I wouldn't have taken you for a subscriber to the *Reporter*. And if you were, I still wouldn't have taken you for the kind of woman who'd stare at a grainy photo of a man's backside to determine who it belonged to."

"It was identified," she said coolly, "in the caption."

"So you saw the naked backside," he said, "and *then* stopped to read the caption? I wonder if Dave and Becky knew you could be titillated by such things. And then I suppose you read the whole story."

"No, I didn't read—"

"That's too bad," he interrupted, beginning to enjoy this exchange, "because you'd have discovered that in the nature of their deceptive headlines and captions, it wasn't my backside at all, but that of her personal trainer." He grinned. "I was flattered, though, to have been mistaken for an athlete."

She heaved a long-suffering sigh. "I was simply trying to turn down your offer of help because I know that your life isn't…conducive to…"

He loved watching her struggle for the right words. It took the edge off her duchesslike demeanor and added a fluster that she hated and he found amusing. "Yes?"

"To a wife," she said a little loudly.

"But I wasn't asking you to marry me," he said seriously. "I was offering to—"

"I know that!" she said in a harsh whisper. She swallowed and said icily, "I mean that you're too busy to father children." Her eyes closed and color crept up her throat as she obviously realized how that comment could be taken.

He didn't even have to say anything to win that one.

But she seemed determined to get it right. "I mean," she said with great patience, "that your offer to help—however kindly meant—would only complicate your life."

"I meant," he corrected "that I'd like to help you financially, though, of course, I'd be available for whatever else the boys needed."

"Don't you live in Seattle?"

"Yes."

"Well, that's 3300 miles away."

"I have a jet."

"Of course you do."

Okay. Now he was getting annoyed with her. "You seem to resent the fact that I'm successful."

"No, I don't," she retorted. "I resent the fact that you think you can solve all my problems with your genius touch or your money!"

SUSAN COULDN'T BELIEVE she'd said that aloud. He was staring at her in confusion.

She looked for the boys in the play area to avoid his eyes. She saw the kids crest the slide, then disappear down it in a laughing rush.

Aaron reached across the table to turn her face toward him when she continued to ignore him.

"Do you *not* want to take the boys?" he asked with a gentleness that surprised and unsettled her.

Guilt rose out of her chest to strangle her. She had to clear her throat to be able to reply. "I *do* want them! I do!"

"Because you promised Becky."

"Because they need me, and because it's the right thing to do! I'm just...a little..."

"Scared."

"Yeah." There was a certain relief in admitting it, even to him. Then she felt the weight of the trusting child in her arms and knew the three wild boys on the slide needed her, too, even though they didn't understand that. So she pulled herself together. "But that doesn't mean I won't do just fine once I get the hang of it and the boys are enrolled in school and settled into a routine."

She didn't like the way he was looking at her, as though he'd found a chink in her armor. As though she wasn't quite what he'd thought her to be and he was now concerned about his nephews.

She was about to assure him that the boys would be fine with her when the door from the play area flung open and John and Paul tumbled in. They rolled along the tile floor, punching and kicking at each other all the while.

"Paul gots a bleedy mouth!" George announced. He was dancing around his brothers like a referee at a wrestling match. "'Cause John kicked him in the face!"

Susan tried to sidle out of the booth with Ringo still asleep against her, but Aaron was already pulling the boys apart, holding them away from each other with a hand to each jacket front.

Aaron pointed John to the booth and held the wriggling screaming Paul to examine his mouth. He dabbed at it with a clean handkerchief.

"Looks like he knocked out a baby tooth," Aaron

said, lifting the boy into his arms. "I'll take him into the men's room to wash his mouth."

Paul clung to his neck, crying pathetically.

"I didn't do it on purpose!" John shouted after him. "I was coming down the slide after him and he stopped at the bottom and turned around. He got my foot in his face, but I didn't kick him!" When Aaron and Paul disappeared into the men's room, John turned to Susan and said imploringly, "I didn't! It was an accident."

"Yup," George confirmed. "An assident."

Susan dipped the end of a paper napkin in her cup of water and dabbed at a scratch under John's eye. Her life, she thought, had become an "assident."

AARON LISTENED to both sides of the dispute when they got home. Paul was finally willing to admit that it might have been an accident, but was most grieved by the missing tooth. "I don't have a tooth to put under my pillow! That's a whole dollar I don't get!"

"That isn't true." Susan was suddenly inspired. "Didn't you know that you can use the tooth of a comb when you lose the real tooth?"

John, Paul and George looked at each other then at Aaron.

"Is that true?" John asked skeptically.

"Absolutely," Aaron replied. He dug into his pocket and pulled out a small black comb. "And I've got a comb right here. Pick out the tooth you like the best and we'll put it under your pillow."

Paul took the comb and frowned over it. "Do we have to wait for it to fall out?"

Aaron kept a straight face with difficulty. "No. I'll snap it off for you."

He indicated the one at the end, next to the rim. "That one. Then you can still use the comb."

"Okay." Aaron snapped off the tooth with the Leatherman tool in his pocket and handed it to Paul. "Got a handkerchief to put it in?"

"No."

He dug into his pocket again and produced one with a silver monogram. "There you go."

"All right!" George and John followed Paul upstairs to help with the ritual.

"That was a stroke of genius," Aaron said to Susan, reaching down to lift Ringo, who'd walked around the table to him.

Susan flexed her stiff arms. "I've got a million of those gems tucked away for emergencies. So, you can take care of packing up and selling the house?"

"Sure." He looked around the modest fifties-era tract home. It was from the togetherness period when rooms ran into one another without doors. The living room, dining room and kitchen were built around a brick fireplace. "You take anything you want. I'll just close it up for a couple of months until I can come back, look through things and save some stuff for the kids and me. Then I'll sell it."

That sounded reasonable. She pointed to the two guitars hanging above the mantel. "Do you think I could have Becky's guitar? When we were kids she used to con me into singing with her at family picnics, and I can remember swaying with her to the music of that guitar. I know, the kids should have it, but they'll be with me, anyway."

"Of course. Take it home with you when you go."
He glanced down at Ringo and smoothed his tiny
cowlick. "This little guy's a cuddler. He walks pretty
well, but he certainly seems to prefer lap sitting."

"I guess even babies get upset when things change,
and being held is comforting."

Aaron nodded. "True. I've had moments like
that."

"Yes. So have I."

Aaron thought he caught a wistful hitch in her
voice. He was just beginning to really understand
what she was taking on here. "Are you seeing someone?" he asked wondering what this new responsibility might do to a relationship.

"No." She got up and pushed in her chair. "I meet
a lot of men in my line of work, but they're confused
by a woman who can use power tools and carry a
four-by-four. And generally, men are uncomfortable
with women who confuse them." She made a rueful
face. "At least, I think that's why I have trouble with
relationships. Or it could be I'm just funny-looking
or hard to get along with."

"Well, you're not funny-looking," he said.

"Thanks." She laughed lightly and came around
the table to relieve Aaron of Ringo. "I've got to get
some of the boys' things packed. I'll take—"

Ringo began screeching and clutched Aaron's ears.

Susan stepped back in surprise.

"Whoa! Ouch!" Aaron tried to pry the boy's fingers off him, but Ringo only screamed louder. "Okay.
Let's change approach," he shouted at Susan over the
protesting screams. "Why don't I help you pack and
bring him along?"

She looked hurt. "I don't understand. He's always liked me."

Aaron rolled his eyes in false modesty. "Oh, I have this irresistible charisma. Sometimes it's a terrible burden. You're powerless against it, so don't try to fight it. If we were going to be in each other's company long enough, soon you'd be holding on to my ears and screaming, too."

Her hurt feelings fled as she laughed at that suggestive remark. "A carpenter and computer..." She'd been about to say "nerd," but Aaron Bradley was as far from a nerd as any man she'd ever met. "Genius?" she finally finished. "I don't think so."

He looked surprised. "Why not?"

"We have nothing in common." She led the way to the stairs and he followed.

"Having things in common is overrated. It pretty much rules out surprises."

"But surprises can be bad, as well as good."

"True. But you wouldn't rule out the good ones to save yourself from the bad ones, would you?"

She thought about that at the top of the stairs while waiting for him. Ringo had wriggled to get down and Aaron was now helping him climb one laborious step at a time.

"If you're so philosophical about relationships," she asked, "why aren't you in one?"

"Takes a lot of time and energy from business," he said with a frankness she appreciated even as it horrified her. "And I haven't found anyone who'd make me want to do that."

"But..." She watched him supporting Ringo's valiant struggles up the steps and found it paradoxical.

"Do you want your life to be just about business? I mean, I know you have an active social life, but if it's all just superficial, is there any satisfaction in that? Any fulfillment?"

At the second step from the top he lifted Ringo by his hands and deposited him on the landing. Ringo giggled triumphantly.

"I get those from my work," he insisted.

She looked up at him in disbelief. "But they're not the same.

"Fulfillment from success tells you that you're good at what you do. Personal fulfillment tells you that you have value *whatever* you do."

"How do you know that?" he challenged with a grin. "You said you didn't have a relationship."

"I've observed others. Dave and Becky, for instance."

He nodded a little grimly. "Yeah, well, Dave and Becky were pretty unique. And I'll only believe you when you can tell me that from firsthand experience."

"Susan!" A loud desperate scream came from the direction of John's and Paul's room.

Susan ran the short distance to find that someone had opened all the drawers in the highboy dresser, and it was tilting forward, threatening to fall onto the boys, who pushed hard against it.

She shot both hands out to help just as a toy dump truck on the top slid off and hit her in the head.

She struggled to maintain her balance while seeing stars.

"Got it." Aaron pushed the top two drawers closed and held them while giving the dresser a solid shove that righted it again. John pushed the other drawers closed.

"Wow!" the boy said excitedly. "I didn't know *that* would happen."

"Hey!" Paul held up the truck. The scoop had snapped off. "Susan's head broke your truck!"

"What did the truck do to you?" Aaron pulled her hand away from the top of her head and a trickle of blood fell onto her forehead and the skin in the V of her blouse.

"She's bleedy!" George, reported the obvious.

All six of them crowded into the small bathroom while Aaron wet a washcloth and dabbed at the wound. "You have a cut about an inch long," he said. "But it's not very deep. I think all it needs is a little antiseptic."

The boys crowded around Susan, who sat on the edge of the bathtub. She felt like a subject in an operating theater.

"Can you take your hair down?" Aaron asked, turning to the medicine cabinet. "Your hair's pulled tight and covering part of the cut."

Susan removed the pins that held her hair up and handed them to Paul, who put them on the counter.

Then Aaron was hovering over her again. He reapplied the washcloth, then put it aside and ran his fingers through the back of her hair, probably to move the strands that covered the cut.

But it had the most surprising effect on her.

It felt wonderful. As though it were happening in an elongated moment, she felt the palm of his hand brush the nape of her neck and the back of her scalp, then his finger burrowing into her hair and threading through it to the ends.

She felt the contact in every root. Sensation rippled over her scalp.

"Does that hurt?" Aaron asked.

"Just...a little," she said breathlessly.

"Sorry. Here comes the antiseptic. Guys, turn around so you don't inhale the spray."

The boys dutifully turned around and Susan covered Ringo's face with her hand.

"Hold your breath," Aaron directed, shielding her eyes with his free hand.

He sprayed, the spot stung for moment, and then it was over.

But she retained the memory of his hand in her hair.

Chapter Two

Aaron helped John and Paul pack their clothes and toys, while Susan worked in the younger boys' room. George was helping Susan, and Ringo was down for a nap.

Though Aaron handled denim and fleece, chambray, woolens, cotton and corduroy, he could still feel the silk of Susan's hair on the back of his hand.

This is not good, he told himself.

He didn't know why he'd done it, except that he'd wanted to touch her hair since the first moment he'd seen her in front of the church. The bump to the head had provided him with a good excuse.

He usually allowed himself to have what he wanted because, generally, he didn't want much. He worked hard, gave himself wholeheartedly to his projects and had discovered early on that giving his employees whatever it took to make them comfortable and happy in their work was ultimately best for all of them.

He'd been terrified all the way over here that he'd hate Becky's cousin and wouldn't be willing to leave the boys in her care, despite the will.

But the situation was perfect for him. She was everything the mother of four boys should be. And he thought the fact that she could admit she was a little bit afraid of the future made her seem that much more sane and capable.

All he had to do was see to it that she had everything she and the boys needed materially, and she would do the rest.

This...tug toward her, this fascination with the children he was experiencing were just complex manifestations of grief and guilt.

They didn't really need him, and he had a new product line coming out in four months. He had a lot of sleepless nights and working weekends ahead of him.

He reasoned with himself all afternoon and had himself convinced by dinnertime.

When he went downstairs with the just-awakened Ringo, he was surprised to find Susan in the kitchen making mashed potatoes. The boys watched television in the living room. Crumbled hamburger meat fried in a pan and smelled wonderful. A can of corn waited on the counter.

"You cook, too?" he asked in surprise.

"Nothing gourmet," she replied "but yes, a little. Though seldom for myself. Why?"

"I thought maybe a woman who was into power tools wasn't interested in cooking."

She smiled at him over her shoulder. "Cooking is just construction with food." She dipped a spoon into the mashed potatoes and offered it to him. "Enough salt?"

He tasted. "Perfect."

"It's just shepherd's pie, but the boys like it. I made it the night I got here."

"I opened an account for you at a Princeton bank," he said abruptly, stepping out of the way as she took an oblong pan from a bottom cabinet.

She put the pan on the counter and turned off the heat under the burners. "What? Why?"

He'd suspected he'd be in for objections. "It gave me something to do in San Francisco while I was waiting for the fog to lift. I took care of it on-line."

She began layering corn, hamburger and mashed potatoes into the pan. She paused in her work to look up at him as though wondering what had brought this on. Her brown eyes scanned his face.

"I'm able to support the children," she said calmly. "There's no reason for you to feel obli—"

"Of course there is," he interrupted a little more loudly than he'd intended. "They're my nephews. I want to know that you can keep them in new shoes while they're growing, that there'll be enough money for sport or music lessons or whatever they might want to pursue." He sighed and lowered his voice. "I want to know that you won't be worn to a nub trying to keep it all together."

She laughed lightly as she opened the oven door. "I don't think money can guarantee that, Aaron. But thank you." She put the casserole in the oven and closed the door.

"Susan," he said firmly, "I'm doing it."

"It isn't necessary."

"It is to me."

She set the temperature and the timer, then turned to smile at him. "All right. You do what you have to do.'' Then she moved past him to pull place mats out of a drawer.

Frustrated, Aaron abandoned the argument and asked her when she intended to go home.

"Tomorrow," she said. "At least, I hope so, I'm having a little trouble lining up a truck. But I have a show to film from a room I'm working on at home. You're welcome to come along if you want to spend a few more days with the boys."

He nodded. "Thanks. I appreciate that. I can get a hotel. What time is dinner?"

"Half an hour," she said.

"All right. If you'll excuse me I have a little business to take care of."

"Of course."

He went to his suitcase for his laptop, found a quiet spot and e-mailed the office.

SUSAN SAW INSTANTLY the advantage of having a man at the dinner table. The usual harassment the boys engaged in despite her efforts to guide a civil conversation was quickly squashed by Aaron's frown of disapproval.

"You always hog the butter!" Paul shouted across the table at John.

"Well you *eat* like a hog!" John countered, oinking loudly for full effect as he shoved the butter tub at his brother.

Inspired by the oinking, George contributed excitedly, "I can talk like a donkey!" and proudly brayed at high volume.

"Guys," Susan said quietly, "let's not do that tonight, all right? Your uncle's here and I'd like to think that when he goes home, he'll remember you as having good manners."

Silence fell at the table. John put down his fork.

"You're going home?" he asked grimly.

Aaron nodded. "I have to go back to Seattle."

"Why?" Paul wanted to know.

"Because that's where my business is," he replied, looking a little shaken by their obvious distress. "And my home. And my dog."

George, seated at his right hand, said earnestly, "Susan would let you come live with her. She's taking all of us to live with her. I bet you could even bring the dog." He turned to Susan. "Couldn't he?"

"He can't bring his business," Susan explained, "which is why he has to go home. He has a lot of people who work for him and a lot of people who buy things from his company. They need him there to do his work."

"He could call and tell them where he is," Paul suggested. "If you can't go home, you should always call."

"Right. But this isn't like just being late for dinner. Thank you, Paul." Aaron accepted the butter from him. "This is important work. A lot of people depend on me being there to do my job."

"But I thought you were the boss," John said. "Doesn't that mean you can tell other people to do the work and they have to do it or they get fired?"

"A good boss does a lot of the work himself," Aaron replied. "Or even when other people do it, he sticks around in case there's a problem and to make sure everything's getting done in the right way."

"I know!" Paul shouted, waving both arms in the air. "We can all go with you!"

"But Susan has a job here," Aaron persisted. Susan could tell he was finding their arguments exhausting.

John sighed. "It's too bad we couldn't move New Jersey closer to Seattle."

Aaron patted his shoulder. "You can all come and visit me at Christmas," he said. "How would that be?"

"How long till Christmas?" George asked.

"Nine months, give or take a few weeks."

"That's how long it takes to have baby," Paul chimed in. Then added seriously, "Only you can't do that 'cause you're a guy."

"Well, I'm pretty happy about that," Aaron said with a grinning glance at Susan.

And then for some completely mysterious reason, Paul's mention of a baby and Susan's soft brown eyes watching him connected in his brain in a way that made him temporarily breathless, speechless, mindless.

A part of him was thinking that his mind was working like a teenager's, snatching double entendres out of the air. Another was thinking speculatively, *Hmm...*

"Your uncle has to go home," Susan said gently but firmly, "and we have to let him."

"Why?" John asked simply. "I mean, if we want him to stay with us?"

She obviously didn't know what to say and looked to him for help.

Aaron was just a little offended by her eagerness

to get him out of their lives and let her flounder. It was perverse, he knew, since he kept telling himself he had to get away, but it was the principle of the thing.

"What kind of dog do you have?" Paul asked.

"A Siberian husky." Aaron reached for his coffee cup and saw that it was empty.

Susan noticed and got up to get the carafe from the warmer.

"Those are the ones with the mask," John said. "Jared Butler down the street has one."

George's eyes widened. "There's a dog that wears a mask?"

John and Paul groaned while Aaron explained about the Husky's markings.

Dinner and the conversation about Aaron going with them ended when Ringo, bored with being ignored, threw his plastic bowl from the high chair into the middle of the table. It overturned two glasses of milk and landed with a splat in the mashed potatoes on top of the remaining shepherd's pie.

All hands were required to clean up.

Susan maintained a militarylike schedule to get the boys in and out of the shower, then scrubbed Ringo in the bathtub. Aaron helped her get everyone to bed.

Ringo and George were asleep before the covers were pulled over them.

"So...where are they exactly?" Paul asked. "My parents, I mean. I know they're with God, but where is that?"

"In heaven," John answered. "It's in the sky."

"Like...in a plane?"

"No. In the clouds."

Paul, ever practical, propped up on an elbow, frowning. "But they'd fall out."

John stared morosely at the ceiling. "They have wings."

Aaron was tempted to correct the misconception, but wasn't sure what could replace it. Who knew? And the thought that Dave and Becky had wings and lived in the clouds was somehow comforting.

"Nobody really knows where heaven is," Susan said simply, quietly, "because nobody can come back to tell us, and if they see that we need anything, they tell God about it."

"Like if we wanted to move New Jersey closer to Seattle?"

She sat on the edge of Paul's bed and smoothed his hair. "Like if you wanted to have sweet dreams, and think about happy things like all the fun stuff we're going to do together."

John folded his arms pugnaciously atop the covers. "What if we asked them to come back?"

Susan tucked Paul in, then went to John's bed. "That's something they can't do, John. But they're with us in spirit."

"That's not good enough," he said unequivocally. "I want them back."

"I know," she replied gently. "So do I. But you can't have that."

"Then I want Uncle Aaron to stay."

She patted his arm. "We all have to get on with our lives, John. Your uncle has to get on with his, and we have to get on with ours."

John turned onto his side. "Well, it sucks."

She leaned down to kiss his cheek. When she stood to leave the room, she looked tired and grim.

Aaron felt even worse than that. He kissed Paul, then John. "I know it doesn't seem like it now," he said, "but pretty soon you won't feel so bad and life will be fun again. I promise."

The boys gave him the look children give adults when they know they're being scammed.

"Yeah," John replied. "Good night, Uncle Aaron."

SUSAN SHOOK CEREAL into bowls, added milk, sliced bananas, and told herself bracingly that the day couldn't be too awful. All they had to move was two rooms of furniture—the boys' bedrooms. Paulette Norris, her producer and Chris Charbon, her neighbor, were coming to help her. How awful could that be?

She didn't want to think about it. Keeping four little boys out of trouble while heavy furniture was being moved struck terror into her heart. She'd have to leave Paulette or Chris with the boys while she helped the other move. Or maybe their uncle would stay with them. She wasn't sure just when he intended to return to Seattle. He'd missed the funeral and seen the boys. There was nothing else left for him to do here.

He'd folded the blanket he'd used last night on the sofa and stacked it neatly with the pillow in a corner. He'd apparently left already on some errand he hadn't shared with her, because he didn't seem to be in the house. His bag, though, was at the foot of the stairs where he'd left it.

"I don't *want* to move," John said as Susan spooned instant cocoa into a lineup of cups.

She smiled sympathetically at him over her shoulder. "I know you don't. But most of my television show takes place in the room I'm fixing at my house and it would make things a lot easier for me if I didn't have to travel across town. I think you'll like it once you get there."

"Do you have ponies?" Paul asked.

She shook her head. "No ponies."

"Dogs?"

"Nope."

Paul sighed dramatically. "I don't want to go either."

George looked woeful. "Are we gonna go today?"

She poured hot water into the cups and stirred. "Yes," she said. "My friend is going to stay with you while I move all your stuff over, then we're going to have a pizza party at my house, then you can fix things up in your room however you like."

George's lip began to quiver. "But I don't want to go today. Can't we go tomorrow?"

She took the handle of two cups in each hand and carried them to the table, wondering what she could do to lighten the mood. Only Ringo happily stuffed cereal into his mouth, unaware that his brothers' world had crumbled—and that they weren't too happy with the woman who was trying to reassemble the pieces.

"We have to go today," she explained gently "because I have a show to do the day after tomorrow and I have a lot to get ready."

John poked desultorily at his cereal. Paul picked up spoonfuls of milk, then tipped the spoon and dribbled it back into the bowl again.

George began to cry.

A firm rap sounded on the door, followed by Aaron's arrival in the room. He was wearing jeans and a dark blue sweatshirt that seemed to change the color of his eyes. He was followed by two other men, one of them pushing a furniture dolly.

One of the men Susan recognized as Micah Steadwell, whom Aaron had introduced to her in front of the church.

"Hey guys!" Aaron said to the boys. He smiled at Susan. "I got some help and a truck. We should have the job done in no time. You remember Micah," he said to Susan.

"Of course." She returned Micah's smile. "Good morning."

Micah drew a tall good-looking man forward. "This is my brother, Ross. Ross, this is Susan Turner, Aaron's friend."

The man offered his hand to Susan. He had dark hair and laughter in his eyes. "I'm pleased to meet you. You're somewhat of a legend at Hardware and Muffins."

She blinked. "I'm...where?"

"Hardware and Muffins. My parents' hardware store—my mother runs it alone now. She was inspired one day to put a coffee bar in the back and all of a sudden it's become the place to be in Princeton."

"No kidding." Susan smiled, hoping she didn't look as confused as she felt. Coffee and books, sure. But coffee and hardware?

He seemed to understand what she was thinking. "Once you meet my mother, you'll understand," he said clearly convinced that was true. "She's unique."

Micah smiled. "That's the nice word for it."

Ross went on. "She has classes for women on working with tools called Hardware for Women. She stocks Legacy, you know. She's wanted to invite you to come and speak to her group for months, but she was sure you'd be too busy." He glanced beyond her to the boys, who were watching the adults with a little less despair than they'd shown earlier. "That's pretty much a certainty now, isn't it?"

Susan shrugged. She loved talking to women about what she knew best. The critics claimed that her show was so successful because she demonstrated carpentry and fix-it projects for women without talking down to them, while encouraging them to take on bigger and more complicated jobs. She made it seem as though she was having one-on-one dialogue with each woman in her audience.

"Maybe when I get better organized..."

Ross smiled broadly. "Great! Because there's an inherent bonus in talking to Mom's group."

"What's that?"

"There's a Daddy Club meeting going on across the shop at the same time."

"A what?"

"The Daddy Club," he explained, "is a group I formed for single fathers needing help dealing with their children. We have men who are changing diapers and staying up all night with teething babies, and others who are going through the minefield of raising teenagers and staying up all night waiting for them to come home. But you'd have free child care while you're talking to the ladies, because we've just turned part of the stockroom into a playroom full of toys and games, and we dads alternate supervising.''

Susan tried to take it all in. A self-help group of single fathers holding meetings in a hardware-and-muffins store where women were learning to work with tools.

Micah smiled at her perplexity. ''It works, believe it or not. You'll have to come and see.''

Susan was beginning to believe that she would.

But for now, she had to deal with Aaron Bradley and his propensity for taking over.

She raised an eyebrow at him. ''It's very nice of you to bully your friends into helping,'' she said politely, ''but I've got it covered. *My* friends are coming to help.''

As she spoke, Paulette and Chris arrived, stepping into the living room and studying with interest the collection of men.

Paulette wore black tights, a baggy black sweater and hiking boots with black socks. Her luxuriant blond hair had been pulled into a ponytail on one side of her head, giving her a frivolous look very much at odds with her television savvy.

Chris wore green velour sweats that highlighted rather than concealed her diminutive proportions. Bleached blond hair was cut short around a wide-eyed gamine face.

All three men turned and stared.

Susan made introductions, noting with a hint of disappointment that now that she had four little boys following her everywhere, men would never look at her the way these men studied her friends. Then she admitted to herself with bleak candor that they'd never looked at her that way *before*.

Aaron turned to Susan his eyes alight with amusement. "This is your idea of a moving crew?" he asked.

"They're my friends," she replied, a little annoyed with the question. "And they're busy. I went for loyalty, not muscle."

"I beg your pardon," Chris interrupted, walking up to Aaron, her eyes filled with amusement, also, but mingled with pride. "I run a fitness center."

Aaron gave Chris a smile that caused the smallest flutter in Susan's chest. She chided herself for her absurdity. The smile hadn't even been directed at her.

"But furniture has to be carried, not run on," he said pointing toward the stairs. "Why don't *you* direct, and we'll be the muscle?" He looked over her head at Paulette. "Or did you want to direct, too?"

Paulette laughed. "No, no. Chris can direct. I'm just here to look pretty."

Micah smiled at her. "You're doing a wonderful job."

Paulette tucked her arm in his as they followed Chris and Ross up the stairs.

Aaron crossed to the table and looked down into his nephews' still-troubled little faces. "I bet you're thinking that moving's going to be really awful," he said.

Paul and George nodded. Ringo continued to pick cereal out of his bowl and eat it with great concentration.

"We don't want to go," John said. "Everything's...different."

Aaron picked George up, sat in his chair, then perched the boy on his knee. "But everything's different whether you stay here, or go to Susan's. And Susan's got more room than you have here, and a much bigger yard."

"She doesn't have a pony," George reported.

"Or a dog," Paul added.

Aaron's expression said that he agreed those were severe failings. "But don't you think it'd be cool to have a big swing set with a slide and monkey bars and stuff like that?"

Paul and George looked interested.

"I'm going to order one this afternoon," Aaron said with an apologetic glance at Susan. "And a sandbox for Ringo."

Susan presumed the apology was for not having asked her first. Usually his presumptions annoyed her, but she understood that he was desperate to cheer the boys up, just as she was.

"I can build a shelter over it," she contributed, "so that you can even use it when it rains."

"We have to go to a different school," John complained.

Susan nodded. "Yes, you do." She wanted to add that he'd make friends in no time, but she knew he didn't want to hear platitudes.

"I hate that," he said.

Aaron nodded. "That's tough. But we'll put up a hoop at Susan's—" again that apologetic look "—and get a basketball so you can practice for the team. Maybe a baseball and a glove, too. For spring practice."

Susan remembered the price of the new palladian

windows she'd put in the back of her house, which looked onto the woods, then dismissed it at the sight of the thin smile on John's face. It was fragile, but it was there.

"There's probably not even a park around," John said.

Aha! Finally! A chance to one-up him. "I have three acres," Susan said. "If there's no park and you get a team together, you can play at our place."

She saw the light go on in his eyes.

"Okay," he said simply, then concentrated on his cereal.

"I want a ball and glove, too!" Paul demanded.

"Me, too!" George said.

Aaron nodded. "Balls and gloves for everybody," he promised.

"All *right!*" Paul exclaimed. "Then we'll have a team!"

Chapter Three

They were moved in by lunchtime, and after the promised pizza for the boys and the moving crew, Aaron took John, Paul and George with him to shop for playground equipment. Ross and Micah went along in an advisory capacity, and Paulette and Chris stayed to help Susan remake beds, replace drawers and redistribute toys.

"What do you know about Micah Steadwell?" Paulette asked.

Susan stood on top of a stool, putting away the box of groceries she'd brought from Becky's kitchen. Paulette handed things up to her, and Chris sat on a rug on the hardwood floor playing ball with Ringo.

"Not much," Susan replied. "Just that he owns a nightclub, and that he and Aaron were good friends all through high school."

"You don't know if he was with the rock band the Knights?"

Susan frowned down a her. Ten years ago the Knights had been one of those music groups whose sound and lyrics struck an empathetic chord with young people. Their reputation for hard living, however, made parents mistrust them.

"I don't know," she said. "Aaron didn't say anything about that."

"I think I recognize his face." Paulette handed up a cardboard tub of hot-chocolate mix. "But they all had wild makeup so it's hard to tell. And he seems so... I don't know, mature, I guess."

"Ten years can make a big difference in someone's life," Chris offered. In her distraction, Ringo's large colorful ball hit her in the face. She pretended to glower at the little boy, who laughed with delight. "Especially in your twenties. How old is he now?"

"I'd guess middle thirties." Paulette handed up a box of crackers. "He did tell me he's single and that he's pretty busy with the club. I'd take that as a warning that he doesn't have time to date but he flirted with me all morning. I don't know what to make of him."

"Maybe you'll just have to see what develops." Chris reached out to catch Ringo's throw. "I'm not usually one for subtlety but if he has a wild past, that's not a very safe bet today."

Paulette nodded, clearly lost in thought.

"But you," Chris said to Susan, "have no doubt what you have on your hands."

"Four little boys leave little to wonder about."

"I'm not talking about the boys." Chris lifted Ringo into her arms and carried him to the counter, where Paulette and Susan worked. "I'm talking about that most dangerous and appealing of God's creatures, the macho male who is too good at heart for you to be upset by his take-charge tactics."

Susan rapped a knuckle lightly on Paulette's head. She came out of her thoughts with a start to hand up a cake mix.

"He does annoy me," Susan corrected, putting the box away, "and I don't find that quality at all appealing."

"He got the moving done in half the time it would have taken us."

Susan held on to the shelf and made a face at her. "And whose fault is that Ms. Size Three, Hear Me Roar? If you guys had a little more meat on you—" she swatted playfully at Paulette's ponytail "—and a little more serious approach to manual labor, I'd have had a more impressive-looking moving crew. They wouldn't have been able to laugh at us."

"They stopped laughing," Paulette pointed out, "when Chris carried the campaign dresser in all by herself."

Chris rocked from side to side with Ringo, shrugging away any glory for the feat. "The drawers were out. It was a cinch. But I think it's rotten that you two stuck me with the one married man among the three."

Paulette made a scornful sound. "You can wrestle them to the ground. You don't have to charm them like we do. You deserve a handicap."

"How long is Aaron staying?" Chris asked Susan.

Paulette handed up cereal.

Susan stepped off the stool to the counter to reach the highest shelf. "I'm not sure," she said, holding on to the door as she put the cereal away. "Maybe tonight."

"I thought he was staying to put the playground equipment together."

"I can do that."

"But the boys seem to really like him. He might want to hang around awhile just to…you know, be here."

Susan sighed. "That's true but that isn't going to help me much when he leaves and does his usual three-year disappearing act."

Susan held her hand down for the next box, and when nothing was forthcoming, she looked down wondering if she'd have to nudge Paulette again. But Paulette wasn't there. And neither was Chris.

She turned carefully on her perch to see Aaron standing behind her, hands on his hips as he looked up at her, his stormy eyes telling her he'd heard everything she'd said. Behind him the boys played excitedly at the table with what looked like new Matchbox cars, Ringo in possession of a big plastic truck. Paulette and Chris stood together on the other side of the room, looking concerned.

Susan wasn't sure what made her lose her balance—the embarrassment of having been overheard speaking her mind, guilt over having condemned a man who'd offered nothing but kindness since he'd arrived, or the simple physics of a body occupying too narrow a space.

Whatever the reason, she was suddenly flailing and trying to turn the fall into a leap, because Aaron seemed to be making no move to catch her.

His hands left his hips just as she'd braced herself to break both legs, and he caught her against him, one arm under her bottom, the other at her back.

She half expected him to fall backward but he caught her firmly. They stood for one protracted moment, his steely arm under her backside, his hand clutching her thigh, his breath warm against the soft skin exposed by the V neck of her sweater.

Then he let her slide down his body until her toes touched the floor. She felt every muscle he possessed from neck to knee.

She didn't want to look into his eyes, but she didn't want to be cowardly, either. She'd said what she felt and, right or wrong, she had to stand by it.

She raised her eyes to his and saw not the anger she'd expected but a sadness she couldn't entirely understand. Somehow it made her feel even worse.

"Tomorrow," he said in an even tone of voice, "we'll get you a taller step stool."

Paulette and Chris excused themselves, and as Susan walked them to the door, Ross, Micah and Aaron carried the jungle-gym boxes into the backyard.

Paulette hugged her. "You're sure you're going to be okay for Friday's show?"

Susan nodded. "Sure. I don't know what I'll do with the boys yet. I'm not putting John and Paul in school until Monday."

Paulette smiled. "Maybe we can work them into the show."

Susan looked doubtful. "I don't think so. Too many power tools. Too much potential for on-air disaster."

"But we film. We can work it out."

Chris gave Susan a hug. "Just tell him you didn't mean it and you're sorry."

"I did mean it," Susan said defensively. "I just didn't mean for him to hear it."

Chris studied her with a furrowed brow. "It isn't like you to be so judgmental. Your father was a flake. That's a different thing from someone who's spending every waking moment trying to build a business."

Cut to the quick because Chris was right, Susan followed her to her van and said tightly, "Family should always come first."

"He's here, isn't he?"

With that, Chris and Paulette climbed into the green van and drove away. Susan went back into the kitchen to find George and Ringo playing happily with their trucks, but John and Paul were not at the table.

Susan went to the French doors and saw the boys helping the men pull the long wooden pieces of playground equipment out of the boxes. Off to the side on an even stretch of grass between the garage and the large shed she used as a shop, Aaron was spreading sand presumably to give the boys a soft spot to land in case of a fall.

Even as she defended herself in her mind, she admired the fact that he'd thought of everything.

She opened the doors. "Do you need tools?" she asked no one in particular.

Aaron didn't even look up at her.

Micah pointed to a long metal box. "I keep a toolbox in my truck," he said.

She nodded. "Hot coffee?"

Micah and Ross replied in the affirmative.

A short while later she carried out three mugs and placed them on the edge of a nearby planter. Aaron offered a perfunctory thank-you while concentrating on attaching the seat of a swing to the chains.

The set was up by dusk, and Susan put on the outside lights in the back so that Aaron could supervise a test of the equipment.

She made a chicken-noodle casserole from a recipe she'd found in Becky's box, put together a salad and baked a tube of refrigerator biscuits.

Micah and Ross left when it appeared that the equipment was sound. So that Aaron didn't have to leave the boys, Susan walked the men to Micah's truck and thanked them for their help.

Ross left her a business card for Hardware and Muffins, and Micah told her that she was welcome as his guest at the Knight Club if she ever needed an evening away from the boys.

She waved as they drove away.

The boys had to be dragged in to eat half an hour later, their cheeks pink, their eyes bright. This was a very different group, she thought, from the boys who'd sat around the table at breakfast, despondent about having to leave their home.

She knew she had Aaron to thank for that.

"You don't have to go tonight do you?" John asked as they ate ice cream for dessert.

Surely Aaron would look at her now. He hadn't met her eyes since she'd turned around on the countertop to find him standing there.

Before he answered John, he would have to know if she would offer to let him stay.

"You said," John reminded him, "you were gonna buy Aunt Susan another step stool tomorrow. So you're not going home yet, right? That means you have to sleep someplace. And this is our house now, too, so we can invite you to stay here.'' John looked to Susan for confirmation. ''Right?''

Aaron did meet her eyes then, but the small yet friendly connection they'd made yesterday was gone. It was like looking into the eyes of a stranger—one who didn't particularly like her on first impression.

She had to look away. ''That's right,'' she told John. ''The sofa in the family room opens up.''

''See?'' John said eagerly.

Aaron nodded. ''Then I accept your invitation,'' he said.

Susan began clearing the table, and the boys helped, falling into a routine she'd apparently already established at his brother's house.

Wanting to help without actually being in contact with her, he wet a couple of paper towels and washed Ringo's face and hands, then cleared the front pocket of his coveralls of noodles. He freed him from the high chair and washed it off while the toddler ran his colorful truck over Aaron's feet.

The table cleared and the dishwasher doing its work, Susan took the boys into the family room and handed John the remote.

''You can be in charge of it,'' she said ''but you have to try to be fair about what you watch, okay? Everybody should have a say in it.''

''Uncle Aaron got us some videos.'' John held up a paper bag.

''*Harriet the Spy* and *The King of Egypt*.'' He studied the remote. ''So I press TV/VCR then Play, right?''

''Right.'' Susan glanced back at Aaron. Fortunately

Ringo was busy trying to redecorate his face, so he didn't have to meet her gaze. He hadn't decided why he didn't want to. Either he was angry with her because he knew he should have made more time to spend with Dave and his family and he'd been plagued by the guilt of it since he'd learned Dave and Becky had died. Or he just didn't like what looking at her did to him. Her large brown eyes seemed to demand, as well as condemn, though he didn't think she was even aware of that.

It was as if he had something she needed, and it was in her eyes every time they shared a glance.

But he had a business to run that was becoming more and more of a rebellious child every day. It was growing bigger and smarter and seemed to require more careful and attentive management.

He couldn't play with the guys in Research and Development anymore. He had to keep his eyes on the money, the numbers, with the competitors looking for takeover and the government looking for mistakes.

And Starscape represented his whole reason for being, the light he'd seen at the end of the interminable tunnel of his childhood, the success for which he'd worked so hard, the proof that his stepmother had been wrong and he *was* worth something, after all.

He couldn't care for a family and keep his business, too. It had to be one or the other.

"It's time for his bath."

He came out of his thoughts to find Susan studying him with puzzlement, her hands on the child he held in his arms. "Unless," she said, as though trying to figure out why he held on to Ringo for dear life, "you'd like to give him a bath yourself. But I warn you—you'll need a wet suit and a snorkel."

She smiled.

He didn't want to respond to it, but it took every fiber of his self-control to stop himself.

"You do it," he said, letting her take Ringo. "I'll supervise the film festival."

Hurt flickered in her eyes, then was gone with a tilt of her chin. "Okay. There's more coffee in the pot. I'll be at least a half hour."

"Take your time."

They were halfway into the film when she returned with sweet-smelling Ringo in footed blue pajamas. She held him out to his brothers, who hugged him good-night, then to Aaron.

Ringo clung to Aaron's neck as though he had no intention of ever letting go. Aaron finally carried him upstairs and helped Susan tuck him in. She turned on a music box on the dresser and handed him the scruffy bear he often toted around by the foot during the day.

In a moment Ringo was rubbing his eyes sleepily and yawning. He didn't seem to notice when they crept out of the room.

Susan stopped Aaron halfway to the stairs. She looked both defensive and apologetic. "I'm sorry about that remark," she said. "You've done a lot for the boys since you've been here and they…we all appreciate that."

He turned to her, hands in his pockets, expression remote. "Really. You made it sound as though all my being here has done is intensify your problems because eventually I have to go."

"I'm sorry," she said, her voice rising a little in agitation. "It's just that helping them through the loss of their parents has been hard, but your being here has helped a lot. John barely spoke until you arrived. But you have to go home and…they lose again. I feel inadequate to the task of making them understand."

"Maybe I should just take them with me." He'd entertained that thought before he'd seen her in action with the boys. Now he wondered if that was what she wanted from him, if that was the need he saw in her eyes. She was young and alone and had her own demanding career.

She gave him an impatient look. "How could you possibly care for four little children?"

That made him defensive. "The same way you will. I'm sure I'd be awkward at first, but they respond to me and that's a start."

"They'd never *see* you."

"I'd hire a nanny."

Her eyes darkened and pinned him in place. "You might remember that I was given custody. It's what your brother and Becky wanted."

"I understand that," he replied patiently, "but the job's too big for one—"

"Who said the job was too big?" she demanded. "Did I say that? No, I didn't. I just said that I felt inadequate, but that doesn't mean I won't do my damnedest to see that they're loved and cared—"

He raised a warm gentle hand to cover her mouth. "You're shouting," he said quietly, the suggestion of a smile turning up the corners of his mouth. "I wasn't questioning your determination or your willingness to do the job. I was just wondering whether any one person should have to do it alone.''

She caught his wrist and pushed away his hand, but his index finger slid over her lips in the process. The sensation seemed to ripple all over her body.

''The reality is that I am alone.'' She spoke firmly so that he would have no doubt about her conviction to see this through. ''I'm sure once we're all settled into a routine, once they've made friends at school and gotten acquainted in the neighborhood...''

It was as she spoke, her color high, her eyes bright with maternal fervor, that he saw the need in her eyes take on a complexity he hadn't noticed before.

She needed him—out of the picture.

So that was it. As difficult as the task of mothering the boys would be, she *wanted* to do it alone. Of course. It was so much easier to move forward when you didn't have to consider anyone else's input.

''Tomorrow we'll get whatever you need for yourself and the boys,'' he said, ''then I'll get out of your way.''

She frowned. ''I didn't say you were in the way.''

''You didn't have to. So I presume it'll be all right with you if I just show up every three years or so?''

He knew that was nasty, but he was feeling nasty. She'd completely misunderstood what he was trying to do here and he just couldn't figure her at all. So even though they had four little boys in common, it didn't look as though they were going to find a way to come together on anything.

She sagged visibly. ''I said I was sorry about that. I'm defensive about people who come and go in other people's lives, because my father did that. He built bridges in Africa and Central America. I know what it's like to be on the receiving end of love that's only intermittent.''

"Maybe the love was constant," he suggested after a moment. "It was just that the nature of his work only allowed you to see him intermittently."

She shook her head. "All the child knows is that he's never there. And after you've waited months and months and he finally arrives, you suddenly realize that he's going to be gone again before you know it. I don't think children should have to live like that."

"I had no children when I embarked on this life. And it's not like I go thousands of miles away. I just go to work."

She nodded. "But the result is the same. Your family never saw you and they missed you."

She was right. Guilt rattled inside him.

"Why don't you relax for the rest of the evening?" he said, moving toward the stairs. "I'll get them going on their showers after the movie."

She opened her mouth to protest that he'd been working hard all day, but he cut her off with a wry, "It's your last chance. I'm leaving tomorrow afternoon. Go on. You must have something to do to get ready for your show on Friday."

It was for the best, she knew. Her real life with the boys would include only the five of them, so the sooner they adjusted to that reality the better off they would all be. It was only right.

She just couldn't decide why it felt so wrong.

Susan heard the wind pick up around two in the morning. It whispered in the trees behind the house but within minutes had grown to a roar. Branches scraped against the house and the windows; she heard the trash can at the side of the house fall over, the chimes on the patio tinkled as though trying to play some up-tempo jazz piece.

And then she heard the first rumble of thunder. It was in the distance, low as the crackling of paper.

Oh, no. She hated electrical storms. She had no childhood trauma to trace it back to, no logical explanation for the serious fear that built in her when thunder rattled overhead and made the house shake.

It wasn't hereditary because her mother had always slept through them, surprised to hear in the morning that there'd been a storm.

She remembered sitting in the middle of her bed as a child, knees pulled up to her chin, eyes closed against the flashes of light as she rocked herself and waited for the storm to end.

The second clap of thunder came, considerably closer and therefore louder.

"This is ridiculous," she told herself firmly as she swung her legs to the floor. She was a mother now. She couldn't cower in the middle of her bed. She had to check on the boys, bring in the chime before it woke the whole neighborhood, put the trash can in the garage.

A peek into the rooms showed the boys still sound asleep. She adjusted blankets, tucked in feet, then left both doors slightly ajar as she ran downstairs to haul in the chimes.

As she did so, a brilliant flash of lightning lit the sky and she hurried back inside, the bamboo tubes riotously noisy in her hands. She closed the doors and put the chime on the dining-room table.

But she wasn't fast enough to cover her ears before the clap of thunder struck, louder, closer, reverberating long enough to laugh at her attempts at courage.

But she made herself function. The trash can. She had to bring in the trash can.

She opened the kitchen door into the garage and reached to the side for the light switch—and collided with a solid object trying to occupy the same space.

Shock was followed instantly by terror. She screamed as a hand reached out to catch her arm, the sound bloodcurdling even to her own ears.

"Susan, it's me!" Aaron said, flipping on the light. He was still holding her arm, looking as though she'd alarmed him as much as he'd alarmed her.

She stared at him, unable to speak.

"I heard the trash can rolling around," he explained, "and I thought I'd better bring it in before you had to chase it into the next county. I'm sorry I frightened you. I didn't realize you were up."

"It's all right," she whispered, her heartbeat choking her. "I...didn't know *you* were awake."

Light filled the dark house like sunshine, then was snuffed in an instant as thunder crashed and rolled, the noise deafening and interminable.

Susan wasn't sure whether to cover her ears to block the sound or her mouth to hold back the scream. She decided to cover her ears and bite her lips.

Aaron flipped off the garage light, stepped into the kitchen and pulled the door closed.

"Are you afraid of—?" Lightning flashed and

thunder struck again, sounding as though a truckload of cymbals had overturned on the roof.

All pretense of courage gone. Susan wrapped her arms around Aaron's chest and held on. It helped considerably when he enfolded her, providing a haven against the next barrage of sound, and the one after that.

SEPARATING HER FROM HIM, Aaron speculated with a smile in the darkness, would probably require surgery. She was holding him so tightly, it felt as though she would join him in his skin if she could, as though their bodies may already have fused in a few places.

"I don't like...thunder," she said against him in a quiet moment, her fingers still clutching the back of the T-shirt he'd pulled on with his jeans.

He ran a hand gently between her shoulder blades. "And I thought this was just a very bold seduction," he teased.

She raised her head long enough to give him a scolding look, then lightning flashed and she buried her face against him again as the harsh sound followed.

He noticed she was trembling and felt sure it was due as much to her mid-thigh-length nightshirt as it was to her fear of the storm.

He swung her up into his arms and carried her to the sofa bed in the family room. He sat down with her and pulled the blanket over her.

"You're probably thinking," she said in a frail voice, "that it's ridiculous for a grown woman to be afraid of thunder."

"No," he said. "I was just wondering if you're warm enough."

She sighed and let her head fall against his shoulder. "I'm fine. You're very warm."

"Mmm." Actually he was getting a little hot. Hotter than was really safe under the circumstances.

"I can't believe this hasn't awakened the boys," she said. "They were sleeping soundly when I checked, but it wasn't this bad then."

"I'm sure they'll come looking for us if they wake up."

"Are you comfortable?" she asked.

That was a tricky question. His body was comfortable. The blanket covered him, too, warding off the nighttime coolness of the house. But the softness of her in his lap, the loop of her arms around his neck, the silken skin of her cheek against his throat was making him decidedly *un*comfortable.

She wasn't his type; he'd concluded that already. And she considered him a failure at familial relationships.

But his traitorous body seemed unaware of that. It was reacting to a scenario going on in his brain that involved stretching out on the soft sofa and making the best of a promising situation.

Then she lifted her head off his shoulder and looked into his eyes at the same instant that lightning lit the room. He saw that complicated need in her worried gaze.

And he realized he'd been wrong earlier when he'd thought that she needed him out of the way.

It wasn't that at all. It was that she'd *wanted* him out of the way for some reason he didn't entirely understand, but she really *needed* him to stay. He felt it in the arms around his neck, in the trusting inclination of her body against his.

Suddenly he had a clearer understanding of her. He seemed to be feeling the very same things, only in reverse.

Whatever this was between them, he didn't need it. But he realized now in the quiet darkness that he wanted it.

He really wanted it.

Chapter Four

Aaron felt Susan's heart beating against him. She seemed to be looking for something in his eyes. Or perhaps she'd found it and was trying to understand it.

He sighed, accepting the inevitable.

"Yes," he said, brushing away a strand of hair caught in her eyelashes. "I'm staying."

Pain shot into her eyes. "I don't want you to stay," she whispered, her voice halfhearted and completely unconvincing.

"Yes, you do. You don't *want* to want me to, but you do."

She repeated that to herself, then frowned at him. "And how would you know that?"

"Your heart's beating against mine," he replied. "It's calling my name."

She rolled he eyes. "Hearts do not call. I don't hear anything."

"It's not a sound," he said. "It's a readout. In your eyes."

She closed them then and groaned, leaning into his shoulder again. "You're misinterpreting," she insisted softly. "It's just because I'm afraid the boys won't ever respond to me the way they do to you. They're guys, after all. Hard to understand."

He chose not to tell her that entangled in her need for him because of what he could do for the boys, he'd read a need that was for her alone.

He laughed. "We're not that complicated. We just want to be loved, obeyed and fed deli sandwiches."

She laughed, too. "Funny. Those are the same things I want." Then, her voice growing serious, though she didn't look up at him, she added, "Really, Aaron. You can't leave a gazillion-dollar company to stay here and hold our hands while we adjust."

For the first time since he'd started working in his garage in high school, he thought about taking a month's vacation without suffering separation anxiety. He put it down to the surreal way one's mind worked in the middle of the night.

"Yes, I can," he said firmly. "I'll stay for a month, help you get the kids in school, chip in with cooking and housework and whatever you think we have to do to help them adjust. Then I'll feel as though I've made up in some way to Dave and Becky for not being around more."

She groaned again. "I wish I'd never said that."

"Doesn't matter. It wouldn't make it any less true."

"I had no right to comment on your life."

"The fact remains."

Thunder had been rolling consistently while they talked and now rattled overhead like sheetmetal.

She flinched against him. From upstairs came a loud anxious call. "Susan!"

George's voice.

Then another call. "Uncle Aaron!"

That was Paul.

Susan scrambled off Aaron's lap and went to the doorway. "I'm com—!"

She got no farther. The sound of running footsteps interrupted her and was followed by the launch into the room of four little bodies, John carrying Ringo.

They piled onto the sofa bed without invitation and snuggled into Aaron, pulling the blankets over themselves. Fear turned to giggles at the presence of adult protection.

Susan studied the crowded sofa, accepting that her comfortable spot in Aaron's arms had been usurped by four needy little boys. She went for the multicolored quilt folded in a big basket in the corner. Her intention was to simply spread it over Aaron's left side where Paul, on the other side of George, was barely covered with the edge of the blanket.

But Aaron took George onto his lap and pulled Paul in closer. "Come on, guys," he said. "Your aunt needs a little room, too."

Paul stood to let her in, then unceremoniously sat on top of her as she spread the quilt.

Aaron put an arm around her shoulder, and tousled Paul's hair. "You guys comfortable?"

She had Paul's bony knee in her stomach, but he'd climbed into her lap of his own accord. She understood that fear had generated this affection, but she didn't care. For the first time since she'd assumed their care, she felt as though they were connecting.

"We're fine," she said. "You okay, George?"

"Yeah."

"John?"

"I'm okay," John replied, "but can you take Ringo, Uncle Aaron? He weighs a ton."

Without waiting for an answer. John placed the drowsy toddler on Aaron's shoulder next to George, then leaned his head on his uncle's upper arm.

"Can you breathe?" Susan asked Aaron. George had an arm pressed to his throat and knelt on his knee, and Ringo had his thumb in his mouth and worked Aaron's earlobe in his fingers like the silk on a blankie.

"Barely." Aaron made a dramatic strangled sound. John and Paul laughed.

"You're *sure* you want to stay?" Susan asked.

John raised his head and smiled up at Aaron. "You're gonna stay?"

"For a month," Aaron replied. "Just to help everybody get adjusted."

"What's adjusted?"

"Ah...feel comfortable. Find your place."

"Oh." John leaned back against his arm. "This place right here is pretty good."

Susan closed her eyes and leaned her head against Aaron's left arm. *Amen,* she thought.

"HELLO?" A FOGGY MALE voice said. "Who is this?"

"Wake up," Aaron said into his cell phone, smiling as he imagined his second-in-command sprawled in the bed in the executive apartment on the fourth floor of the Starscape building. Ted had been living there for the past three weeks, since his wife had locked him out of the house. "It's your boss."

Aaron heard a groggy laugh. "Sophia?"

"Idiot. It's Aaron. When are you going to tell her you're sorry?"

"I'm not sorry."

"So say it, anyway."

"There's a principle at stake here. What do you want, anyway? It's five o'clock in the morning. You still in New Jersey?"

"Yeah." Aaron walked to the French doors and looked out onto the swing set he and Micah and Ross had assembled the day before. "Ted, I'm going to stay for a while."

There was silence for a moment.

"Excuse me," Ted said "but I thought I heard you say you were going to stay for a while."

"You did. For a month."

Another silence. "Did the cousin turn out to be a beast you can't leave the boys with?"

Aaron laughed. "No she's pretty great with them and seems very determined to make a home. But I think I ought to stay around and help for a bit."

Another silence. Ted always thought before he spoke. Except where Sophia was concerned. "Sure," he said finally. "Everything's going well. I don't foresee any problems. But in our twelve years working side by side...I mean, you're *never* gone. You're sure everything's all right? Well, stupid question. Of course it isn't all right. You lost your brother. But I mean—"

"I know what you mean Ted," Aaron interrupted. "I just have to do this."

"Then do it and don't worry about anything here. We're fine. If I have any questions about anything, I'll call you."

"Great. Ted?"

"Yeah?"

"Make up with Sophia. It's all too short, you know? Principles at stake, or not. Call me on my cell phone if you need me."

"Right."

AARON'S HOUSEKEEPER answered on the second ring. "I warn you," she said, her voice sharp and clear despite the hour, "if you are calling to encourage me to change my long-distance service, to contribute to a charity I've never heard of or to breathe heavily in my ear, I have friends in the Public Utilities Commission."

Aaron laughed. "You do not."

"Well," Beebee said. "Now you take pleasure in waking an old woman at five-fifteen in the morning simply to contradict her. Aaron Bradley I'm disappointed in you. But how the hell are you?"

"I'm fine, Beebee. How's your arthritis?"

"The same. Why couldn't you have started a business in Phoenix or Miami, instead of Seattle?"

"How's Burgie?"

"Off his food just a little. Misses you, I suppose. There's no accounting for taste. And I, of course, can't throw the Frisbee far enough, so he considers me inferior company."

"Well, you'll have to practice," Aaron said, "because I'm staying here for a month."

There was that silence again.

"How are the boys?" she asked, her tone softening. Sometimes he forgot that his acerbic old friend was a mother herself.

"They're doing very well," he replied. "Their aunt is kind and smart and very devoted to them. But four little boys is an enormous job, and I thought I should try to help them all adjust. She has a cable-TV show, so I can cut her a little slack to get her work done, at least until she gets the kids into a comfortable routine."

"Hmm. Is she your type?"

"No."

"There really isn't a type you know, when Cupid strikes."

He knew that was true, but it wouldn't be good for Beebee to know he knew. "Cupid doesn't get to New Jersey. If you need anything before I get back you've got my cell phone number, or call Ted."

"Ted's still living at the office, you know."

"Yeah. I just talked to him."

Aaron heard footsteps on the stairs.

When the storm had finally abated last night, he'd carried the sleeping boys upstairs one by one, covered Susan with the quilt and watched her from the safe distance of a chair across the room.

It hadn't helped. He still wanted her.

At about seven-thirty, he'd gone upstairs to shower, then come down again to make his phone calls.

"The kids are coming down to breakfast," he told Beebee. "I've got to go."

"You're cooking?" she asked, clearly horrified.

"Yeah," he replied defensively. "Simple stuff."

"Doesn't she cook?"

"At about the same level of skill that I do."

She tsked. "And the poor babies having just lost their parents."

"Thanks, Beebee," he said. "Don't hesitate to call."

"Do the pair of you a favor and hire a cook!"

"Bye, Beebee."

He tapped off the phone and took out milk and eggs for French toast just as John and Paul careered into the kitchen like little vehicles without brakes.

SUSAN AWOKE STRETCHED OUT on the sofa bed, all by herself. There was a pillow under her head and the blankets had been spread over her. A wonderful silence reigned in the sun-filled room.

For one brief moment she wondered if she'd dreamed it all—the phone call, the children, the funeral. Aaron.

Then she saw toy trucks all over the floor and a "sippy" cup on the coffee table and knew it was all real. Only this delicious silence was an aberration. Someone had closed the door.

She let herself absorb the stillness for several glorious extra minutes, then forced herself to her feet and opened the door. She heard the children's laughter coming from the kitchen, along with Aaron's deep voice.

Before she faced the day, she let herself remember the events of last night, the way he'd held her without recrimination, then told her she had a readout in her eyes that said she needed him.

She put a hand to her face and felt her temperature rise, certain it was true. She'd always needed someone she didn't have. When she'd been a child, it was the father who came home so seldom and always seemed excited about leaving again.

But when she'd become a teenager, she'd begun to dream about the boy who could accept her for the wood-shop monkey she was and want to cherish her, anyway. But he hadn't existed.

As a woman she'd maintained the dream, only given it a man's face and qualities. And, at least so far, he hadn't existed, either.

Until now.

But this was only for month. Aaron was fulfilling an obligation to his brother through his nephews. In April he'd be gone.

It sounded as though the boys were at the breakfast table, so she wouldn't have to feed them. Bless Aaron. He'd be handy to have around—even temporarily.

She drew a breath and straightened her nightshirt so that she could say good-morning, then make a quick run through the kitchen to the back stairs to take a shower and change her clothes.

She had to prepare for tomorrow's show, and if memory served, the sunroom from which she'd hosted the past four shows was filled with boxes, toy-car tracks and various other toys too big for the boys' room or the crowded garage. She had her work cut out for her.

She padded in her socks into the kitchen, only to stop in embarrassed surprise. The boys were at the breakfast table, all right, but so were three women she'd never seen before in her life.

One of them, a sixtyish woman with short white hair and a smile as bright as the sunlight, stood and came to where Susan had stopped. "My God it's *you!*" she said, throwing her arms around Susan, then stepping back to look her up and down. "Adorable even with your hair mussed and wearing a nightshirt and kneesocks." She turned to the other two women at the table. "Do you believe that anyone could look this good when they've just climbed out of bed?"

Susan's eyes searched the room for Aaron and found him making a fresh pot of coffee by the counter. He smiled at her, looking as though he sympathized with but enjoyed her confusion.

"Susan, this is Ruth Naomi Steadwell, Micah's and Ross's mother," he said, gesturing with the filter. "And these ladies are Darcie O'Grady—" he pointed to a pretty freckled woman with curly brown hair "—and Elaine Steadwell." A gorgeous blonde. "Elaine is Ross's wife."

Susan smiled, aware of a desperate need to tug on her nightshirt and hide behind Ruth Naomi while crab-walking to the stairs.

"Hi," she said. "Welcome. I…ah…would you excuse me while I go upstairs and ch—"

"Nonsense!" Ruth Naomi pulled off the dark blue cardigan she wore and wrapped it around Susan's shoulders. "We heard about the rough night you had. You just sit right down here next to this handsome little fellow." she squeezed a lawn chair between the chair she occupied and the one on which George knelt over a large chocolate-chip muffin. Chairs, Susan noticed, had been hauled in from several other rooms. "We brought you breakfast from Hardware and Muffins in the hope that we could bribe you into filling a hole in the programming tonight."

"Tonight? I have…"

"A show to fill tomorrow," Ruth Naomi put in for

her. "I know. Aaron told us all about it. I don't know
a thing about television, but you always make things
look so easy! Do you know I put a medallion in my
dining room ceiling after you showed us how on one
of the October shows? And I couldn't believe how
easy it was. I'd been asking Ross to do it for ages,
but now that he and Elaine are married and have three
children between them, well..." she apparently saw
no point in explaining what that meant in terms of
Ross's free time.

"And Micah." She rolled her eyes. "He can't even
hammer in a nail. Brilliant. Charming. Give you the
shirt off his back. But don't ask him to do anything
handy."

While Ruth Naomi spoke, she forked a fat golden
muffin that smelled of peaches, put it on a plate Aaron
handed her, cut it in two with surgical precision and
applied a generous amount of butter.

"There you go, love. Canned the peaches myself.
We wanted you to see what's offered when you come
to speak at Hardware and Muffins. Aaron's anxious
to sit in on a Daddy Club meeting." She turned to
Aaron, who carried a steaming mug of coffee to Susan's place at the table. "Aren't you, Aaron?"

"Yes, ma'am," he replied dutifully.

"Micah told us all about what a computer whiz you
are." In praise for his cooperation, Ruth Naomi patted
his cheek. "Maybe you could look at my cash register
while you're there. It's been..."

The woman went on, Darcie and Elaine smiled
sympathetically across the table at Susan. She smiled
back, thinking that she was doomed as far as evading
the Hardware and Muffins talk went. And if this muf-

fin was any indication, it might not be such a terrible fate, after all.

When everyone had finished eating, Susan excused herself to get dressed and returned to find that everyone had moved to the sunroom to look around. Ruth Naomi was peering inside a window seat Susan had built under small-paned windows she'd also installed.

"Is anything more charming than a window seat?" Ruth Naomi closed it again, then sat on it. "That's it. That's what you should talk about tonight. If there's anything you need for the demonstration, I can supply it. Lumber, hinges, nails, glue."

That would be easy enough. "I have everything," Susan said. "But it would be easier if I didn't have to haul the lumber."

Ruth Naomi stood decisively. "Great. Give me some dimensions, and I'll have it ready when you arrive. Meeting's at seven-thirty, and be sure to bring the boys. The Daddy Club needs them to practice on."

Susan followed Ruth Naomi as she leaned into the fireplace. "I'd have thought a bunch of single dads would have enough children to work with."

The older woman straightened, running a hand over the rough wood mantel. "They do, but they should know what it's like when all the neighborhood kids come to visit. It's good for them to know how *not* to be overwhelmed. You put in the fireplace, didn't you? A December show. I remember because you hung stockings from it when you finished."

Susan blinked. "I did."

"I remember trying to find a place in the house

where I could put a fireplace, but there just isn't room. And I do have an efficient furnace.''

''Maybe you should put one in Hardware and Muffins,'' Susan suggested.

Ruth Naomi spun on her, staring.

Susan backed up a step. ''I mean, if there's room. Sounds as though you…do lots of chatting and exchanging of thoughts and ideas. It'd be…cozy.''

Ruth Naomi put a hand on Susan's shoulder. It landed like a four-by-four. ''That is inspired!'' she declared. She turned to the young women who'd accompanied her. ''Isn't that inspired?''

They nodded in unison.

''Maybe,'' Elaine suggested ''you could have Susan do it. She might even be able to get Hardware and Muffins into the show.''

Susan remembered the condition of her sunroom and had a sudden inspiration. ''How would you feel,'' she asked Ruth Naomi ''about me filming at your store tonight, provided I can get a crew together a day early?''

Ruth Naomi was speechless, but only for moment. ''I'd *love* that! What do you need? What can I do?'' she demanded anxiously.

''Nothing yet. I'll call my producer and see if we can put it together. I'll call you in an hour or so. Is that all right?''

''Oh, it's more than all right,'' Naomi said, giving her a hug. Then she hugged down the line of little boys standing stiffly in awe of her hurricane-force personality. ''You're all going to be such a wonderful addition to the Daddy Club.'' When she reached Aaron, she gave him a hug, too.

"He spent a lot of time at our house when the boys were in high school," she told Susan. "We wanted him to move in with us until he'd finished, but he was so independent."

Susan wasn't entirely sure what that remark suggested, but she noticed a tightening in Aaron's jaw.

Ruth Naomi said her goodbyes and handed Susan a business card.

Elaine told her that the Daddy Club's auxiliary was having a potluck in the meeting hall at the park. "A week from Sunday," she said. "We have indoor games for the kids if it rains, and the whole park for them to play in if it's nice. We'd love to have you."

The boys were jumping up and down at the thought of a picnic, so Susan was forced to nod. "It strikes me as funny, though," she said "that a club formed to help single men cope with their children has a female auxiliary."

Darcie laughed. "Well, Elaine and I have done our share to get the Daddy Club members married off." she smiled at Aaron. "Might be risky for you to come if you're a confirmed bachelor."

He indicated the boys. "I'll have my bodyguards with me."

It was a playful harmless suggestion, but Susan experienced a curious sense of loss at the thought of him meeting some pretty young thing. Who would she turn to the next time it thundered?

Paulette liked the idea of filming at Hardware and Muffins, and assured Susan that she would scope out the store herself and collect the crew. All Susan had to do was appear with her project.

Susan hung up the phone, thinking that sounded

easy. But next on her agenda was shopping with four little boys.

TWO ADULTS, THREE CHILDREN and one baby seat did not fit very comfortably into an imported compact, Susan discovered. Had the boys been any bigger one of them would have had to be strapped to the roof.

Despite the confines of the car, the boys seemed to consider the shopping trip for a step stool and more groceries a great adventure.

They were brought to attention in the parking lot of the grocery store. Susan, pulling Ringo out of his seat, saw George jumping and dancing right into the path of a red pickup driven by a teenage boy apparently adjusting his CD player rather than watching the road.

She shouted George's name at the same moment Aaron caught him by the collar of his coat—an instant before the pickup would have hit him.

"A parking lot," Aaron said loudly, leaning over George, "is just like a street. The same rules apply— you never *ever* step out without looking both ways first!"

George, mistaking the lecture for anger rather than concern, burst into tears.

Aaron ran a hand over his face, then picked up the four-year-old and balanced him on his hip. "I'm not mad at you," he said more quietly, "but I'd have been pretty upset if that truck had hit you. You have to be careful, okay? That's your responsibility." Aaron turned to John and Paul, who stood back silently. "You understand? When we go out, we stay together. And you never run out into a street or a parking lot without looking. Everybody got that?''

John and Paul nodded vehemently.

Aaron drew a breath. ''All right,'' he said, striding off toward the store. ''Let's go find some good stuff.''

John and Paul ran after him and Susan followed with Ringo, thinking grudgingly that Aaron had done that very well.

They took two carts, the two smaller boys riding in the child seat in each, John and Paul pointing excitedly to everything in a colorful box.

''Can you make meat loaf?'' John asked Susan. ''I really like meat loaf.''

''Yeah,'' Paul seconded, ''with scalloped potatoes.''

Susan turned to Aaron, who followed with his cart. ''Can you make meat loaf?''

''Do we have a cookbook?''

''Yes.''

''Then I can make meat loaf.''

''Scalloped potatoes, too?'' John asked hopefully.

''Those come in a box,'' Susan said, heading for the rice-and-grains aisle. ''We can make those.''

John looked doubtful. ''Mom didn't use a box.''

''Your mother was a better cook than I am, John.''

''Can you make blueberry pie?''

''No, but I can buy blueberry pie.''

John nodded, apparently considering that preferable to not having it at all.

At the meat counter, Susan turned to Aaron again. ''What do we need besides hamburger meat?''

''Breadcrumbs, I think.''

''An egg?''

"Maybe. We've already got those."

Paul watched her put the meat in the cart. "Can we have it tonight?" he asked hopefully.

"Tonight we're going to Ruth Naomi's store," Susan replied, "to do my show. So we're going to have something easy like soup. How about tomorrow night?"

"Okay," Paul agreed. "I like Ruth Naomi, but she kinda scares me, you know?"

Aaron laughed. "Amen," he said quietly.

Chapter Five

Aaron considered a wooden step stool with a pullout step in the houseware aisle, then finally bought a molded plastic one that the boys could also manage without danger of pinched fingers. He stood by tolerantly while each boy tested it, Ringo included.

There was a threat of mayhem at the toy display when each boy fell desperately in love with something he couldn't live without. Susan was braced for it; this happened every time they went shopping for anything. She was about to remind them that Aaron had bought them all trucks yesterday and that he'd put a lot of expense and effort into their new playground equipment when he said, "We're going to a sporting-goods store for your balls, bats and gloves remember?"

They whooped and jumped like wild things.

She loved seeing them so happy, but she was afraid there might be a dangerous principle at work here.

"You can't buy them everything they want," she said, after he'd given the boys quarters to ride the coin-operated horses by the door. She and Aaron stood side-by-side at the checkout while their groceries were scanned and bagged.

"I can if I want to." he took a credit card out of the inside pocket of his jacket. "And I want to."

"Their parents wouldn't have done that," she said gently.

"Their parents," he reminded her "aren't here. I don't believe a little cushion against that reality can hurt them."

She turned toward him and lowered her voice when the clerk glanced interestedly at them while weighing a bag of pears. "When you leave, I won't be able to do all those things for them. And if you've gotten them used to—"

"Yes, you will," he interrupted, also quietly, "because I've opened a checking account for you at the Bank of Princeton. We have to take you there to sign the signature card." He reached into that pocket again and pulled out a brown leather checkbook with the bank's symbol tooled in one corner.

She opened the book and had to take hold of his arm to remain upright. The opening balance was in the low six figures. No wonder the bank put the book in a tooled leather wallet.

"Are you insane?" she demanded in a high whisper.

"No, I'm rich," he replied. "But sometimes those are similar states."

"That'll be..." the clerk announced a total that was about five times more than Susan's usual grocery bill.

Aaron swiped his credit card through the countertop debit machine and completed the transaction.

Susan tried to hand back the checkbook. "There is no way," she said, "that I am taking this from you."

"It's not for you," he said pocketing his receipt. "It's for the boys."

"Money can't make up for—" She stopped abruptly when he turned to her, his eyes darkening with anger.

Two young men pushed their carts out into the parking lot. Susan was forced to follow them to open the trunk while Aaron gathered up the boys.

Susan locked the trunk and thanked the young men, then watched as John, Paul and George stopped deliberately at the road that ran through the parking lot, looked exaggeratedly left and right, then ran toward her while Aaron followed with Ringo in his arms.

Susan opened the back door, noticing as each boy climbed in that he had a small clear plastic ball that contained candy and a toy. She remembered the vending machine near the horses by the door.

Aaron, she was sure, had done that just to spite her. She cast him a glance that said so. It was blocked by his angry glance in return.

With Ringo secured in his car seat, she closed and locked the door and started around to the driver's side.

Aaron caught her arm and backed her up against the car, then braced his arm on the roof on either side of her, effectively boxing her in.

"We have to settle a few things," he said.

She opened her mouth to repeat that spoiling the boys wasn't going to do anyone any good, but he stopped her from speaking with a shake of his head.

"I'm going first," he said, "so please just listen.

Then you'll have your turn." He paused to draw a breath and looked up at the sky as though to collect himself, then began tightly, "I'm not trying to buy the boys' affection, if that's what you're suggesting. And I'm not trying to assuage my guilt—at least not with money. I should have made more time for Dave and his family and I'll always regret that I didn't. I don't think anything will ease that for me. What I'm trying to do is show them that even in the grimness of losing their parents, they're still considered so special that they can have a few things just because they want them. 'Lost your mom and dad? Get a baseball bat and glove.' Seems like very little compensation to me."

Susan didn't even try to speak while he shifted his weight and drew a breath. She just stood in the confined space his body and the car created and waited for him to go on.

"I put that amount in the bank account because your grocery bill has easily quadrupled, there'll be school fees, clothes, lost jackets, all kinds of things we probably can't even imagine, and sometimes when I'm working, it's hard to find me. And I know many families get by on a lot less, but I don't want you to have to, and since it's within my power, I'm going to see that you don't." He expelled a gusty breath and looked into her eyes. "Stop second-guessing my motives. I'm not trying to buy them or make them care for me more than they care for you, so you can relax about that. I think we should spend this month trying to work together to make them feel secure and happy, instead of fighting each other over how that should be done."

She waited. When he seemed to have no more to say, she asked stiffly, "Is it my turn now?"

He pushed himself away from the car, then stood beside her and leaned back against the door. "Yes," he said wearily, "it's your turn."

"I wasn't questioning your motives," she said staring across the lot at the tops of cars. "I was questioning your tactics. But—" she sighed and put a hand to her eyes "—now that you've explained it, I guess you're right. Maybe I am overcompensating for my lack of mothering skills by trying to analyze every move I make. And—" she gave him a dry sidelong glance "—every move you make, too. I'm sorry."

"From what I've observed," he said, turning to look at her, "you make a lot of good moves instinctively. You're doing fine."

The window in the back door rolled down and John's head appeared between Aaron's hip and Susan's waist. "Are you *still* talking? Can we open the bag of cookies?"

"No," Aaron said. "We're going to lunch."

"Okay but if we don't go till you're done talking, we could all starve."

Aaron reached behind him to push John's face back inside the car. The boys laughed.

Lunch was chaotic, but the boys seemed to have a great time. They decided on a buffet, and the boys were thrilled with all the choices and the ability to fill their own plates.

In light of her decision to relax and try to employ Aaron's philosophy of just letting the boys have fun, she tried not to think about the nutritional qualities of their meals. But she monitored her own, especially when Aaron brought her a slice of carrot cake.

"I can't eat that!" she protested.

He raised and eyebrow. "Why not?"

"Because. I had a peach muffin for breakfast."

"This is lunch."

"I know but I used up the day's calories before I even got to the chicken!"

He frowned at her. "I thought you were going to relax. You're going to be so busy chasing kids you'll easily burn everything you eat. Anyway, you can play ball with us this afternoon. We'll keep you running."

When they arrived home, they made a bag brigade from the car to the kitchen table, passing in ten bags of groceries and four sets of balls, bats and gloves, one of the large colorful plastic variety for Ringo.

"Can we go play now?" Paul asked, glove already on.

Susan would have let them, but Aaron pointed to the many bags. "If we're all going to eat, we all have to help put things away. You guys do the canned goods in that bottom cupboard."

While Susan put meat away in the freezer, she glanced over her shoulder to see the boys tossing cans in a relay. Ringo watched from the safety of the playpen, beating the rails on the sides with his new bat.

When everything was finally put away, Susan folded the bags into a plastic box in the pantry. The boys were wild with eagerness to go outside.

"You ready?" Aaron asked her.

"I have to check with Paulette. You guys go ahead."

"I thought you had to work off the carrot cake?" Aaron teased.

She frowned. "Am I wearing it already?"

His eyes slid to her hips, the glance lingering and appreciative. "Okay, make your phone call. I'd hate to see you lose an inch anywhere."

He ran outside with the boys and Susan dialed the phone, inordinately pleased with his compliment.

Paulette had everything under control and told her *Susan's Workshop* was filming at seven-thirty at Hardware and Muffins.

"The only thing different," she said with a brisk tone Susan picked up on immediately, "is that we're doing it live."

"Live?" Susan shrieked.

"Live," Paulette repeated calmly. "*Quilting with Camilla* is always live on Thursday nights—don't ask me why. Anyway, she seems to have the chicken pox and the slot is empty."

"But, I can't—"

"Yes, you can. When Mr. Jekel realized Ruth Naomi has the largest stock of Legacy Tools in Princeton, he thought we should plug you in live tonight rather than use a filler."

Susan groaned. "Let me guess. The Legacy people are in town or something."

"Close. They'll be at the trade show in New York next week. Mr. Jekel's trying to make a few points, and I'm sure we'll make a few, too, if we help him. Come on. You have great presence. This will be good for you."

Good for you, Susan thought after she'd agreed and hung up the phone. That was the line that usually preceded the administration of foul-tasting medicine or punishment of some kind.

AARON DIRECTED the cleanup after a dinner of soup and sandwiches, while Susan showered and changed.

He heard her footsteps on the stairs, and she appeared suddenly in the kitchen doorway in snug jeans and a flannel shirt, neatly tucked in. Her hair stood up in all directions and she held a brush in her hand.

Her cheeks were pink, her look frantic.

"Aaron," she said quickly, "could you and the boys get the boxes near the door in my shop and put them in the car, please? My hair won't *do* anything!"

"Ah...sure." Aaron tried not to stare. She looked like some very sexy dude-ranch Medusa.

She tossed him a key. "Want me to take Ringo up with me?"

Aaron shook his head. "We'll be fine. Keep working on your hair."

She turned and ran back upstairs. He smiled, finding something touching in the fact that she's taken on four boys without flinching, but was so upset about her hair.

"She's only gonna saw wood and hammer nails," Paul said, looking up at Aaron with perplexity. "Why's she worried about her hair?"

John elbowed him. "'Cause she's gonna do it on television, stupid!"

Aaron pointed the boys to their jackets on the pegs by the door to the garage. "No name-calling, okay? And women are always worried about their hair, whatever they're doing." He pulled Ringo's jacket on him, then carried him out to the shop, the other boys trailing him.

He flipped on the light and found himself in the middle of a shop Tim Taylor of television's *Home Improvement* would have found impressive. It had every hand tool and every power tool he'd ever heard of and a few things he couldn't even identify.

In the middle of the room was a large worktable. A gilded picture frame lay on it, clamps holding one side in place. The room smelled of wood chips, paint, linseed oil and...Susan's floral perfume.

"Wow!" John said, picking up a nail gun and looking into the barrel. "I can't believe she knows how to use all this stuff."

Aaron, on the brink of heart failure until he realized the nail gun wasn't plugged in, took the tool from the boy and put it down. "Why? You know she has a television show about using tools." He put Ringo down in an empty cardboard carton. "Paul, you want to keep an eye on him while John and I take this box to the car?"

Paul looked disgruntled. "I want to carry a box."

"Well, you and George can carry the next one."

Appeased, Paul knelt beside the box and made faces at Ringo while Aaron and John carried the box to the garage, George bouncing along beside them.

"It's just that Aunt Susan's not like most girls," John said, picking up their conversation. "I mean, she cooks pretty good, but not like my mom did. Or like that lady that came this morning. But she can use all this stuff that guys use and most girls can't."

"That's because she's special," Aaron said, "and not ordinary."

George jumped up and down like a little piston while Aaron unlocked the trunk. "I think she's pretty!"

"I didn't say she wasn't pretty," John said defensively. "I just think it's weird that she has a guy's job."

Aaron put the box into the trunk then started back to the shop. "A lot of people today think there aren't girls' jobs or guys' jobs. Some men stay home and cook and take care of babies while their wives have jobs because it works out better for them that way. Anybody can do anything if that's what they like to do."

"Would you do that?" John asked.

"What?"

"Stay home and cook and take care of babies?"

"Ah... I suppose I could as long as I had a computer."

Aaron and John waited with Ringo, who now had the empty carton on top of him and was playing peekaboo, while Paul and George carried a small toolbox to the car.

"Is that what you're going to do for a month?" John wanted to know. "Cook and take care of us?"

"Yep, that's it."

"What happens when you go home?"

"By then," Aaron replied, "you'll be used to all this new stuff and everything won't seem so hard. You won't need me to be here like you do now."

That seemed to mystify John. "But what if it thunders again? Who're we gonna sit with? Susan was shaking last night. I don't think she likes it, either."

Aaron was saved from having to answer by the

sudden arrival of Susan into the room. She'd pulled on a short fuzzy jacket with bears and green trees on it, and her hair had been plaited into a single braid at the back of her neck and tied with a red ribbon.

He wasn't sure why braided hair should take his breath away.

"Do we have everything?" she asked, checking the corner where now only the big toolbox remained.

"I'll get that," Aaron said.

"Where's Ringo?" she demanded, turning in a circle.

"Ta-da!" John said, whisking the box up to reveal the toddler, who laughed with delight.

Susan scooped him up. "Okay, let's go."

HARDWARE AND MUFFINS was a large brightly lit store, well equipped and efficiently set up, as Aaron expected of anything Ruth Naomi owned and operated.

Everything imaginable was stocked in wide aisles that led to a coffee bar at the back of the store.

Several women of Ruth Naomi's vintage were already gathered near rows of chairs set up nearby.

Cameras, lights and crew were everywhere.

Elaine Steadwell was there to greet them, and she showed Aaron and the boys where to put Susan's things.

Susan took the boys into a huddle. "You be good, okay?" she asked. "Be polite, mind your manners and be quiet during the meeting when people are talking."

"No need for all those instructions." Ross appeared and took Ringo from Aaron. "We've got a sitter tonight. Because of the show, we're holding the Daddy Club meeting in the lumber barn. There's an empty storage area there the kids can play in. Come on, guys.''

"Be there in a minute," Aaron promised, then turned back to Susan as Ross took off with the boys. "Are you going to be okay?" he asked.

"Yeah. I think so.''

He smoothed the turned-up collar of her shirt. "Why are you nervous? You do this all the time, don't you?"

She made a face. "Not live, I don't. And I just don't feel quite like myself anymore. There's so much I don't know. I mean, Elaine and Darcie are both gorgeous and feminine and accomplished cooks, and I'm this shop rat…''

"Susan." He put a hand to her face and turned it toward him as she looked around in agitation. "They didn't ask you here to talk about cooking. They want to know what you know about window seats. And you're pretty gorgeous yourself, shop rat or not.''

She blew air between her lips in a very ungorgeous way. "I am not.''

"Well, let's not get into a you are, too, I am not argument. What do you mean, you don't feel like yourself?"

She shrugged. "I'm not sure. I'm confused about the boys a lot of the time, but I know I can do it and I really want to. It isn't that. But I feel sort of… I don't know. Jumpy? Like I want something I can't quite identify." She laughed suddenly. "I'll be fine. Just going live is scary. I'm okay. You'd better go. Pay attention to the meeting because I'm supposed to go to New York a week from Friday to host the Legacy Tool booth at the Hearth and Home Show.'' She winced suddenly. ''I forgot to mention that, didn't I?''

She was going to leave him alone? ''Yes, you did.''

''Susan!'' Ruth Naomi blew in with her usual force-five intensity, gave Aaron a hug, then absconded with Susan.

The Daddy Club meeting, Aaron thought, looked like a bunch of guys gathered for Saturday-afternoon football, only on folding chairs, instead of recliners and sofas. The chips and dips were there, the pretzels and the popcorn, but they drank coffee, instead of beer in deference to the children in the next room.

Ross introduced the guest speaker, Neil Graber, a behavioral psychologist from Princeton University who was probably his age and seemed very mellow.

He began his talk by explaining that his wife of twelve years was now somewhere in the Himalayas on a search for self and had left him with two little girls, three and five years old.

Some of the men, who'd apparently been similarly abandoned, nodded their understanding.

He said that for the sake of his daughters, he'd chosen not to be bitter, but to do his best to learn how to cope with his difficult situation.

The nods weren't quite so enthusiastic.

''Easier said that done, to be sure,'' he went on. ''But I didn't want my daughters to learn bitterness, and children are learning from you every moment of their lives, even when you think they're not aware.''

He finally invited anyone who had a problem with his children to offer it to the group for discussion.

They were thirty minutes into a lively discussion on how to help children express anger when there was a disruption in the next room, followed by the laughing escape of several of the smaller children, George among them.

"Kelly! Karen!" Graber shouted from the podium.

Aaron could only guess as he ran in pursuit that the two blond little perps who accompanied George were Graber's daughters. A man who'd been introduced to Aaron as Bill Swanson came running out of the storage room, colliding with Aaron and Graber.

"I'm sorry!" he said anxiously, clearly stressed and upset. "I happened to mention there'd be muffins later, and when I turned around to find another book to read to them, the little ones were gone!"

Aaron pushed him back toward the room. "Stay with the other kids. We'll get them."

But they'd lost valuable time over Bill's explanation.

The door to the main part of the store was just closing on the escapees when Aaron and Graber cleared the barn's door.

"Oh, no," Graber groaned. "With a live show in progress!"

Aaron picked up speed, Graber on his heels—and found himself surrounded by lights and cameras before he could bring himself to a stop.

Graber collided with him.

SUSAN WAS NOT entirely surprised that disaster loomed on the horizon of her first live show. She'd expected it. Known it would end her show and possibly even her career.

Her wood cut for the window seat and her holes drilled, she'd been just about to move the project into Ruth Naomi's office for assembly when three little bodies joined her on camera.

And two large ones crashed into each other like a pair of Keystone Kops in contemporary dress.

"Hi, Susan!" George said loudly. Then he turned to the camera and with unabashed charm declared to *Quilting with Camilla*'s usual audience, "I'm George!"

The ladies of the Hardware for Women audience laughed.

Susan caught Paulette's eye and got a sympathetic half smile, but also a rolling index finger that meant "Keep going!"

"Well." Susan lifted up the smaller of the two girls who'd accompanied George. "We may as well introduce everyone. What's your name, sweetie?"

"Kelly Emily Graber," the child replied. "I'm free!"

Susan smiled at the camera. "I don't think she's saying that she and her friends have escaped from the Daddy Club meeting. I believe she's telling us that she's three years old. What's your friend's name, Kelly?"

"Karen Louise Graber," the other girl shouted. "I'm five! I'm her big sister."

"The children are here," Susan told her viewing audience, "with their fathers because Hardware and Muffins provides a meeting place for the Daddy Club, a group of fathers who get together to help each other deal with single parenthood. While we're building projects on this side of the store, they're building families on the other.''

Kelly pointed to Graber. ''That's my daddy!''

Susan put the child down and drew Graber closer to the camera. ''This is Neil Graber,'' she said ''who's a guest speaker at tonight's meeting. Tell our audience about yourself Mr. Graber, and the subject of tonight's meeting.''

He slid Aaron a plea for help, but Aaron backed out of camera range, beckoning George to him. But the boy was too fascinated with the spotlight.

''I'm Neil Graber. I teach behavioral psychology at Princeton.'' He smiled suddenly, apparently deciding the situation required a little humor. ''And I'm going to go against all the rules and yell at my daughters as soon as we're off camera. They were apparently bored with my suggestions for dealing with anger in children.''

Susan laughed. ''Maybe that's because they don't seem at all angry. Apparently you know what you're talking about. Let's see if your students were paying attention.''

She beckoned to Aaron.

He shook his head.

''Come on, Uncle Aaron!'' George rushed over to Aaron to take him by the hand and pull him toward Susan.

The ladies laughed. The crew smiled.

''Hi, George,'' Aaron said, then sent a threatening glance at Susan.

Now into dealing with the potential disaster and

determined to make the most of it, Susan challenged him with at smile.

"How does a parent help children express anger, sir?" she asked.

He drew a breath and answered in a tone that belied the blood in his eye. "By loving," he said, "listening and expressing anger in a positive way himself."

Susan nodded, impressed with his calm and concise reply. "Thank you, gentlemen. Thank you, Kelly, Karen and George." she spread an arm to indicate the area around her. "Hardware and Muffins, ladies and gentlemen. Where else can you get building instructions and child-rearing advice under the same roof? Stay with us. We'll be back to finish this window seat right after a word from Legacy Tools."

Loud laughter on all fronts filled the station break. Neil scolded his girls and George chatted with a cameraman.

"You're going to pay for that," Aaron promised Susan with a dangerous smile.

Susan patted his arm. "You were great. And you had the right answer."

He sighed and studied her with an unnerving intensity. "Is there an answer to you, I wonder?" he asked.

WHEN THE SHOW WAS OVER, everyone, audience and crew included, considered it a success despite the disruption.

Ross Steadwell introduced Aaron to Flynn O'Grady, Darcie's husband. He was tall and dark-haired with a strong handshake.

"I can't believe you're here at a Daddy Club meeting," he said to Aaron. "Isn't everyone after your company? I read about you in *Time* magazine."

Ross explained that he'd lost his brother and sister-in-law, and was helping with the care of four boys.

Flynn paled. "I'm sorry. *Four* boys? Without a woman in your life?"

Aaron told him about Susan having custody and his staying around to help.

A stream of children came running at them, followed by Bill Swanson, looking relieved to be free of his duties. Ross led them to tables set up in an alcove where Elaine and Darcie were pouring juice and coffee and putting out muffins.

When Susan finally joined them, Flynn leaned across the table toward her. "When you wrapped up the show," he said, "I heard you talk about the addition you're planning on your house. What did you have in mind?"

Ringo had climbed from Aaron's lap into hers, and she fed him bites of muffin. "I'm living in a great old Arts and Crafts style house that I've done some work on, but I'd like to add another wing to one side, up and down, so that there's more room for the boys. They fit all right as it is, but I think it'd be better if they could spread out a little. And of course, as they grow older, it'll be a necessity. And I can use the projects on my show. I was thinking of hiring an architect and a builder and doing all the finishing work myself."

Flynn nodded. "What if I drew up your plan for a class I teach at the community college? I do good work and it wouldn't cost you anything."

Susan's eyes widened and she turned to Aaron. "What do you think?"

He was shocked that she consulted him. Once he recovered he nodded. "Sounds like a good idea to me." He glanced at the card Flynn gave him. "He has all the right letters after his name."

"Micah can vouch for me." Flynn laughed. "I designed his nightclub."

Ruth Naomi blew by to hug Susan and to tell her what a hit she was. "My phone is ringing off the hook. You have to promise to come back," she said. "That was so much more fun than when the *men* try to tell us how to build things." She said the word with affectionate emphasis. "They teach us how to make planter boxes and put on light-switch covers. But *you* believe we have brains and skill."

"All it takes is attention to the project," Susan said, "and respect for the tools."

"Can you fit us in again one day next month?" Ruth Naomi cajoled. "Even without the cameras?"

Flushed with success, Susan nodded. "I will, I promise."

Flynn tapped the card Aaron still held. "And when you're ready to get moving on this, call me and I'll bring my class out to look over the place and have you tell us what you want to accomplish."

RINGO AND GEORGE fell asleep on the drive home. Susan handed John the house key, then took Ringo out of the baby seat while Aaron carried George.

Within half an hour, everyone was in bed. Conversation came from John's and Paul's room, but George and Ringo never stirred.

Susan went to her bedroom, ready to simply fall across the bed, only to see the bare mattress and naked pillows. She'd forgotten that she'd thrown her bedding into the washer before they went shopping.

With a groan she went to the linen closet for the extra set of bedding, then remembered she'd put it on the bed Aaron was using.

"Problem?" Aaron asked, coming out of John's and Paul's room. He had an armload of laundry he put into the hamper in the hallway. He was handy to have around, she thought absently.

She pointed to her bedroom. "I forgot I was doing laundry."

Aaron peered around the molding into the room. She had an old brass bed, a tall oak dresser, a dry sink filled with plants, a small lace-covered table with a lamp on top and a little farm chair.

The country-style sweetness of it surprised him in a woman who was so forthright and practical.

"We can spend the night together on the sofa again," he suggested, everything inside him softening, warming.

She had that needful look in her eyes, but she was wary, too. "Not a lightning bolt in sight."

"Men and women come together even when it isn't storming outside. Sometimes..." He couldn't stop himself. He went to her, put a hand to her face, saw her eyes widen and her lips part and felt himself draw even closer. "Sometimes," he went on in a whisper as he lowered his mouth to hers, "it's storming *in*side."

God. He'd wanted to do this for days. Her parted lips were soft and cool against his, and though she didn't touch him, she had lifted her mouth to meet his.

He kissed her gently, intending simply to explore what was behind that look in her eyes.

She returned his kiss in the same spirit—interest, discovery—her mouth moving with his, opening, reaching.

He felt the smallest ignition in her, a quickening of interest, discovery under way.

He put a hand to the middle of her back and urged her closer.

She came without hesitation, her arms going around him, her hands barely touching his back.

And suddenly he couldn't stand the hesitance another moment. He wrapped both arms around her and deepened the kiss, pressing her even closer, feeling her breasts flatten against his ribs as feeling billowed inside him.

SUSAN WAS AWARE of being unable to breathe—and discovering that she didn't have to. All she seemed to need were Aaron's kisses. He rained them over her face, along her throat, on the rim of her ear and on her mouth again.

His arms held her so tightly that she couldn't move, but she didn't want to. She felt wrapped in warmth, shielded by muscle, embraced by the strength she'd missed her whole life long.

She moved her arms to circle Aaron's neck, stood on tiptoe to reach for more kisses, letting her body melt with his so that she could absorb the power contained in him.

Then a little voice called, ''Susan? Susan!''

She swam in sensation for another moment, then Aaron opened his arms and she felt desire simply disengage.

Shaken, surprised, confused, she looked into Aaron's eyes, saw the grudging acceptance of disappointment there and turned to the younger boys' room. George was sitting up in bed.

She perched on the edge of it and smoothed his hair. "What is it, Georgie?"

"I just...I didn't know if you were there," he said. He sounded drowsy, as though something had startled him awake.

"I'm right here," she assured him, kissing his cheek. "I'll always be right here."

"Okay." He lay down again and she covered him. "What's for breakfast?" he asked, snuggling into his pillow.

Breakfast, she thought with a mild sense of panic, trying to remember what they'd bought. The film crew would be arriving at eleven and she had to somehow put a show together by then.

"Scrambled eggs and bacon," Aaron said from the doorway. "And English muffins."

"Mmm." George made a pleased sound. "I like English muff..." He was asleep before he could complete the thought.

Susan gave him one more pat, sure he would be able to feel it in his sleep, then went to the crib where Ringo had thrown off his blanket and lay on his face with his sleeper-clad bottom in the air. She eased him down and covered him again.

Aaron stepped back as she walked into the hallway. She was still trembling inside, she realized. Or it had started again when she got close to Aaron. A part of her was still wrapped in the gauzy embrace of his attentions, but another part of her was trying to draw away.

Kissing Aaron wasn't safe. She had too much to do, too much to think about to be distracted like that. And he was leaving in a month, anyway.

She waited for him to try to touch her again so she could tell him they had to remember that they were here for the children and that their feelings didn't count.

But he didn't touch her. He simply stood there in the shadowy hallway, clearly aware that something subtle had changed. It annoyed her that he could read her so well. Her women friends were always complaining that their men never understood them, yet Aaron seemed always to read her mood—maybe even her mind.

"We forgot," she said folding her arms, "that we're here for them. We mustn't do that anymore."

He was silent for a moment, then he shifted his weight and asked, "Does being here for them preclude our being here for each other?"

"Yes."

"Why?"

"Because…there's no future in it."

"How can you say that," he asked, "when there's such an active *present* in it?"

"Because we're dealing with children here. The present isn't what counts."

She knew that was wrong the moment the words left her lips. If she'd had any doubt, his quiet but indignant "What?" would have confirmed it for her.

"Okay that's not what I mean," she corrected quickly. "I meant that when you're dealing with kids, you can't live for the moment, because their futures depend on what we do with ours."

She wasn't satisfied with that explanation, either, but she was finding the concept difficult to put into words.

Still, he seemed to understand.

"How do you know that letting ourselves have the moment," he asked, "wouldn't help us work out the future?"

She looked him in the eye. "Are you going to walk away from your company?"

He met her gaze without flinching. "No."

"Then there you go. My kids are not going to have an absent father."

"We aren't even—"

"I know we aren't anywhere near real relationship," she interrupted hurriedly, "much less at a point where we should be talking marriage, but...the way I feel..."

She stopped herself just short of admitting that her feelings for him were strong enough already.

HE KNEW WHAT she was thinking. He'd always been intuitive. It had made his stepmother's hatred that much uglier, but had been his success in business. It helped him read between the lines in financial news and in conversations. It made him a good reader of the market, a good employer, a good customer-relations man.

He guessed it might make him a good father, even if he didn't have a lot of time to spend at home.

But it didn't seem to do anything for his relationship with Susan except make it more difficult. It would be a hell of a lot easier to go back to Seattle in April if he'd been unaware that she cared for him.

"I didn't build a mulitmillion-dollar company," he said "by being afraid of anything—present or future." He *was* afraid of the past, but it didn't seem necessary to admit that.

"It's not a matter of fear," she said, her chin at an indignant angle. "It's a matter of self-preservation. The obstacles are insurmountable."

"I'm a programmer," he said. "A problem solver. There are no insurmountable problems."

She shook her head. "Now you're just being arrogant."

"I know my limitations." He framed her face in his hands and kissed her slowly, lingeringly. She was too surprised to resist. He raised his head and smiled into her upturned face, satisfied that she'd responded despite her protests. "But I don't have any where you're concerned."

While she stared at him, he went into the family room and returned with a blanket and a covered pillow which he placed in her unresisting hands. I'd invite you to share my bed," he said dryly, "but I never make love to a woman whose first thought is self-preservation. Good night."

Chapter Six

Susan's Friday show on replacing a fireplace surround went smoothly. Aaron took the boys to McDonald's for lunch, then shopping for new jackets for school.

"They don't need new jackets," Susan protested during breakfast cleanup while the boys were getting dressed. "The ones they have are fine."

"But they're going to be the new kids," he argued. "They'll have more confidence if they're wearing something new and cool that makes them feel good."

She eyed him warily. "Nothing in leather with fringe."

"Not for them," he said with a wickedly arched eyebrow, "but would you like something like that?"

She put a hand to her forehead. "You didn't hear a thing I said last night."

"I heard every word." He'd wiped off the table and pushed the chairs in. "Did you hear anything *I* said?"

"Also every word." She handed him a wad of napkins, which he put into the sunflower-shaped holder in the middle of the table. "So we're at an impasse. Isn't that an insurmountable obstacle?"

He inclined his head in a could-be gesture. "To some, I suppose. Not to me."

She started the dishwasher. "I have a show to do," she grumped. "You shouldn't be hassling me. The camera picks up every line."

He looked her over. She wore coveralls this morning over a pink knit shirt, her irritation with him brightening her eyes and coloring her cheeks.

"You look good enough to be stolen away from cable to star in *Baywatch*," he said.

She pushed him bodily out of the kitchen, her color deepening. "Take the children and go," she threatened, "before I do you bodily harm!"

"And you think I'd want to run from that?"

"Go!"

He left with the children at the same time Paulette arrived with the crew.

Surrounded by the familiar trappings of television production, Susan began to relax. Stepping over cables, dodging lights and cameras was comfortably familiar and helped her recapture the woman she used to be before the boys and their uncle took over her life.

Paulette hurried past as the makeup girl gave Susan's lips a little shine. Her producer did a double take and stopped to look. She gave her a thumbs-up. "Looking good, girl," she said. "Having a man around must be—"

Susan felt the threatened return of tension. "Stop it," she said to Paulette, "before you end up with a mike up your nose!"

The makeup girl blinked. Paulette didn't even

flinch. "Good thing you're not doing a show on manners and gentility. See you after the show."

Susan felt calm and in control throughout the show. She didn't know how to explain that, considering what an upsetting influence Aaron had become.

She tried to share that thought with Paulette afterward. They sat at the kitchen table with coffee and the package of Twinkies in the large economy size the boys had pleaded for.

Paulette gave her a knowing look. "I know what it is."

"What?"

"You *like* his upsetting influence."

Susan narrowed her eyes at the woman with whom she'd been through cable hell and high water. "What on earth makes you say that?"

Paulette shrugged. "The fact that your eyes are tired but they still sparkle. The fact that you have more to do in your life than any two women should have to handle, and still your smile is up a few watts. You may be annoyed, but under it all, you're happy."

"He's leaving in a couple of weeks!"

"That doesn't prevent you from enjoying today, does it?"

And where had she heard this argument before? "Yes, it *does*. The boys are not going to go through what I went through with my father."

Paulette frowned. "Honey, they've *lost* their father. I'm sure they'd love to have another one, even if he's part-time. I think what bothers you about Aaron Bradley bothers you as a woman and not as a mother to the boys. And it doesn't bother you enough to wipe the smile off your face, so don't pretend it does. You know what I think?''

''No.'' Susan popped the last bite of Twinkie into her mouth. She was about to add that she didn't care, but she had to chew first and was much too late.

''It's that all your life you've been convinced that the man you wanted your father to be didn't exist. And now you've discovered that he does. And not only is he great with the kids, but he's great with you.''

Susan looked heavenward in supplication. ''Well, Dr. Laura, if that were true, why would I not be hanging on his neck and dragging him to a minister?''

Paulette studied her, then shook her head as though dismissing the question. ''I don't know. Sometimes you're just too complex for me.''

''Oh, come on. I'm an open book.''

''Yeah, right. The tax code, maybe. Can I have another Twinkie?''

''No.''

Paulette and the staff piled into the company van. When they left, an office-supplies truck pulled up and two men unloaded three large oblong boxes about six inches deep and one smaller square one.

One man ran up the walk to the steps. ''Mrs. Bradley?''

''No!'' she denied a little too vehemently.

He looked startled and consulted his invoice. ''Oh. Ms. Turner.''

She relaxed. ''Yes.''

He seemed to relax, too. ''We have the desks Mr. Bradley ordered.''

''Desks?''

"Four of them," he said. "Shall we leave them on the porch or bring them inside?"

Aaron had bought the boys desks. Four boys under eight, and he'd bought them desks!

She opened the door knowing there was no point in resisting. The deliverymen were not the enemy. Not that there was an enemy. Just a very stubborn overly generous pigheaded uncle.

"Bring them inside, please."

When they left, another deliver truck pulled up in front, and a smiling man in brown went into the bowels of the truck and returned with a very large box and a slightly smaller one stacked on top. Judging by his bow-legged walk, the burden was heavy. What had Aaron bought now?

He deposited them on the porch.

"Thank—" Susan began, but he'd already turned back to the truck.

"Got a couple more," he called over his shoulder. He returned three more times with what appeared to be the same-size boxes, then returned one final time with four long narrow boxes. They were all, Susan noted, from Starscape.

She signed the man's electronic clipboard.

"You starting a mail-order business?" he asked.

"No…" Susan didn't understand the question.

"It's just unusual to have four new computer systems mailed to a residence." He winked at her. "You're a bookie, aren't you?"

She nodded. "I have to do something to maintain my computer habit."

He laughed and loped back to his truck.

Susan tried to lift one of the boxes to start bringing

them inside. She concluded the long skinny ones were keyboards; they were easy to handle. The smaller boxes were only moderately heavy in proportion to their size, but the larger ones were hard to lift, even for a woman used to slinging lumber.

Aaron brought the boxes in when he and the boys returned home. The deliveryman had been right; there were four computers—three standard ones in bright colors and a very simple one for Ringo to learn to use one day. The boys were beside themselves with excitement.

While they followed Aaron up and down the stairs with each system, Susan delved into the bags they'd brought home from the Kid Connection, an exclusive children's store.

He'd bought four woolen stadium jackets with leather sleeves, each in a different color. She shook her head at the price tags.

"What?" Aaron asked, reappearing at the bottom of the stairs. "Don't like them?"

"They're great," she assured him with a tolerant smile. "Very cool. But you could have bought a small country for what these cost you."

He ignored that remark and handed her what appeared to be a sheet of instructions. "Do your superwoman carpentry skills stretch to understanding directions written by someone who doesn't speak English? I'm getting nowhere with the computer desks." he offered her a hand up off the sofa. "The only one I've had any success with is Ringo's little one—it just had to be unpacked."

She accepted his hand with a deliberately superior smile. "Let me show you how it's done."

With a deft yank he brought her right into his arms. "I'd like to show you how a few thing are done," he said, nuzzling her ear.

"Uncle Aaron!" Paul shrieked. "George is standing on my television!"

Susan pushed out of Aaron's arms and started up the stairs at a run, unsure whether to be relieved or disappointed by the interruption.

Aaron followed, shouting back, "It's not a television. It's a monitor."

Susan scooped the boy off, relieved to find no damage had been done, at least externally.

She took the two younger boys with her into her room where there was a television to keep them occupied while she assembled the computer desks, ignoring the written instructions and diagrams.

Moving two desks into John's and Paul's room meant stacking the bunk again, but the boys were happy to do that in the interest of their new computers.

By dinnertime Aaron had everything connected and several basic programs loaded. Susan had to pry the boys away to eat, then John, Paul and George spent all evening with Aaron, who was directing their efforts to learn to use the programs.

Susan stayed downstairs with Ringo, who enjoyed her undivided attention while they stacked and restacked colorful blocks.

Saturday afternoon they played baseball in the backyard, Ringo in a playpen with his own plastic ball and bat and other toys. Two little boys John's and Paul's ages from up the road came to see if they could join the game. By the time they left for dinner, the five children were fast friends.

They watched television after dinner, Aaron in the big chair with Ringo and George in his lap. Susan on the sofa flanked by John and Paul. Two large bowls of popcorn were devoured while they watched *101 Dalmatians*.

Susan was a little surprised to find that some of her tension was gone and that she felt…happy.

The boys also seemed content as they leaned against her and dipped into the popcorn bowl without turning away from the screen.

She looked at Aaron. Ringo and George were fast asleep, Ringo with an arm around Aaron's neck. George lay on his back, straddling Aaron's knee, arms and legs splayed.

As though sensing her gaze, Aaron turned to her, his expression relaxed and lazy, an eyebrow going up in question.

"We need a third person," she said, "to get up and make coffee."

He grinned. "You're elected. My guys are asleep."

"But I have to see what happens," she complained with an answering grin, pointing to the television.

"The lady doesn't get to make coats out of them," John replied, looking up at her. "And they find Wizzer at the end. So you can go make the coffee."

"Thanks a lot." she pushed herself to her feet, casting a wry glance at Aaron as he laughed. "Next time, it's your turn."

"I'll make breakfast," he promised.

"It's doughnuts for breakfast tomorrow." She went

toward the door, stopping to put the afghan over the sleeping boys in his lap. "After church."

Aaron winced. "Church?"

John and Paul turned to her in unison, also asking in dismay, "Church?"

She gave Aaron a pointed look as she tucked in the blanket.

"Church," he said on a forced-enthusiastic note. "Good. That'll be good. And doughnuts after. Good way to start a Sunday."

"We never go to church," John said, unimpressed with his uncle's pep talk.

"You have to kneel down in church," Paul groaned as though that were akin to bamboo under the fingernails.

"There's lots of music and pretty-colored windows with pictures in them," Susan cajoled. "You'll like it. You guys need more pop while I'm up?"

CHURCH, AARON GROANED inwardly. His stepmother, Helen, had just about destroyed his belief in any divine power caring what happened to anyone. But it would be good for the boys to believe it.

"I don't want to go," John grumbled when Susan was out of the room.

"But we'll be able to talk to Mom and Dad if we do," Paul said excitedly, that fact clearly just occurring to him. "'Cause they're in heaven where God is, only, God goes to church, too, so we can give him a message."

John considered that a moment, then turned to Aaron. "Is he right about that?"

"Pretty much," Aaron replied. He decided his own reservations didn't count here.

John sighed and accepted the inevitable. "Do we have to wear ties?"

"Do you have one?"

"No."

"Then I don't think you have to wear one."

But Susan did try to comb their hair, the following morning, which resulted in a mutiny.

Aaron was shaving in the downstairs bathroom when he became aware of the sound of shouts and racing footsteps over the hum of his razor. A moment later the bathroom door burst open, and John, Paul and George hid behind him, their dark eyes reflecting some gross injustice.

Then Susan appeared in a blue skirt and silky white blouse, open at the throat. Her dark hair was loose and hung full and glossy to her shoulders. For a moment he was surprised into speechlessness by her blatant femininity—and a desperate need to touch.

But he was drawn out of the spell she cast when John pointed an accusing finger at her from behind him. "Help us, Uncle Aaron!" he begged. "She wants to *spray* us!"

Susan held up the can, her index finger still on the button. "It's just hair spray, guys, not bug spray."

"That's for girls!" Paul objected peering out from around Aaron's hip. He seemed to consider that worse than poison.

"And we're *guys!*" George put in climbing onto the toilet seat to see over his brother.

Susan rolled her eyes. "For heaven's sake." She advanced into the room, spritzing a shot at her own hair to prove her point. "It isn't going to hurt you. It'll just make you look civilized."

The boys drew back. Aaron spread out his arm protectively to shield them. "I'll handle it," he said, loving the look of consternation combined with alienation on her face. She may have a theory about how children should be raised, but he had gender superiority when it came to male stuff. "Guys use hairdressing, not hair spray. We'll meet you at the door."

She looked at Aaron and the three boys and shook her head. "I'll bet baseball players use hair spray!"

John gasped in horror. "They do not!"

She glanced at her watch, then at Aaron. "You have five minutes or we'll be late."

When Aaron had finished, John, Paul and George looked like choirboys. They smiled at their reflections, clearly relieved to have been spared the hair spray. In their good slacks and sweaters they reminded him sharply of their father. He swallowed an unexpected lump of emotion.

"All right," he said, herding them out the door. "We'd better hurry. You know we have to be quiet in church and try not to fidget."

"What's fidget?" George asked.

"Wriggle," Aaron replied.

"But what if I get itchy?"

"If it's on your nose," John said, "you can scratch. But if it's on your butt..."

"Just don't think about being itchy," Aaron advised, "and you won't be itchy. Think about the doughnuts afterward."

He was amazed that his advice worked. The boys were exemplary during the service and were fussed over by the minister when they streamed out of the church.

He shook each boy's hand, then reached up to pat Ringo in Aaron's arms. "Something going on here I should know about, Susan?" he asked, with unabashed inquisitiveness.

John, Paul and George spotted the boys who'd joined their ball game on Saturday and ran down the steps where they all pushed and shoved one another.

She explained about their parents and the will that assigned her custody.

"You've been handed a big job," the minister said.

Susan shrugged. "It seems to be working out."

He smiled at Aaron. "Was she given custody of you, too?"

"I'm the boys' uncle," Aaron answered, offering his hand. "Aaron Bradley."

The minister shook hands. "Welcome, Aaron. I'm glad you joined us this morning. Sets a good example for the boys."

"He's only here because I bribed him with doughnuts," Susan confessed.

The minister laughed. "Your job is to get them here, whatever it takes. *My* job is to keep them interested and make them want to come back. So will I see you next week too, Aaron?"

"You will. I'll be here until the end of April."

"You don't live here?"

"No. Seattle."

The minister patted Susan's shoulder. "Susan's done a lot for the church, you know. She put in the kitchen cabinets in the reception hall and retiled the floor. It was her gift to the church for our centennial. I don't know what we'd do without her."

Aaron wasn't surprised to learn about Susan's generosity. Giving seemed to define her, though she made little of it.

"You go to church every Sunday?" he asked as the boys wandered back and forth in front of the bakery's enormous display cases, wide-eyed with indecision.

"Not *every* Sunday," she said, pointing to a raspberry-filled croissant. The clerk reached for it and put it on a platter next to the glazed doughnut she'd gotten for Ringo. "But I go as often as I can."

"I didn't realize you had such a spiritual side." He pointed to an apple fritter and caramel nut roll. They were added to the platter.

"It's not such a spiritual side," she denied. "It's just hard to work with wood and not appreciate the earth in which it grows and the hand that made the earth."

The clerk smiled sympathetically at Susan. "The boys have decided. They want the chocolate-iced doughnuts. Is that all right?" Susan groaned. "Sure," she said.

Aaron didn't understand the problem until fifteen minutes later when the boys had finished and there was chocolate everywhere—on their cheeks, their hands, in their hair, on the table, the chairs, on Aaron and Susan.

"I wouldn't have thought that there was enough chocolate on four little doughnuts to make this much of a mess," Aaron said, dipping a napkin in his water glass and wiping a streak of chocolate off her cheek as she washed George's hands. The clerk was at work with a dishrag on the tables and chairs.

She shook her head. "I don't know. It's like they operate in a centrifuge and stuff spatters everywhere. Okay, guys. Let's go."

Aaron left the clerk a healthy tip.

"We have to go to school tomorrow," John said morosely as they drove home. "Man."

"I like school," Paul said, seemingly surprised that his brother was upset.

John looked at him as though he was hopeless. "I like school, too, but we're gonna be *new*. All the guys'll pick on us and all the girls will whisper about us."

"That'll just be for the first day," Aaron said, "then they'll get to know you, decide they like you, and you'll be one of them."

"You're sure that'll only take a day?" John asked.

"I'm sure."

"I want to go to school," George said as Susan turned onto her street. "Only, I can't read. But I can write my name."

"You can go to preschool." Susan patted his knee. "On the mornings when I'm busy with work, you can be with other kids."

"Who's that?" John asked, pointing through the car window at the front porch.

Aaron looked—and couldn't believe his eyes. Leaning against one of the porch columns was a tall angular woman in her middle sixties wearing a gray tweed coat under which protruded spindly legs supported by bright red tennis shoes. On her head was a red wool hat with a small rolled brim.

At her feet on one side of her was a battered blue suitcase, and on the other, a beautiful black-and-white Siberian Husky, his head resting on his crossed paws and an expression of boredom on his face.

"Oh, my God," Aaron said.

Susan turned the car into the driveway and asked worriedly. "Why? Who is it?"

"My housekeeper," Aaron replied.

Chapter Seven

Beulah Bernice Pottersby, or Beebee, as everyone called her, had been Aaron's first secretary when he started Starscape. He'd had only half-a-dozen staff then, and two rooms in an old factory-turned-office building on the waterfront had constituted his business office.

Beebee's husband had been a manufacturer's representative, and they'd had two daughters. She'd stayed with Aaron through the lean times, exulted with him when consumers began to notice the easy manageability of his versatile programs and word of mouth quadrupled business in his fifth year.

Then suddenly he was outselling his competitors, bought the office building, and made the cover of *Time*.

At the same time, Beebee's life took a difficult turn. Her husband died, one daughter married and moved away, and the other went off to school. She was grateful for her job, but her own sudden bout of heart trouble made the high-pressure Starscape front office a danger to her rather than a comfort.

So Aaron hired her as his cook-housekeeper and invited her to live in.

She'd accepted his offer—and taken carte blanche to run his personal life. But that didn't explain her presence three thousand miles from the house in her care.

Burgie raised his head as Susan pulled the car to a stop, then got to his feet when Aaron opened the door. He sniffed the air and before he even caught sight of his master, raced across the lawn and around the car to collide with Aaron near the fender, barking gleefully.

Burgie leaped against Aaron's chest, his forepaws resting on his shoulders as Aaron leaned down to hug him and rub his neck. Burgie slurped his face.

The husky barked even more excitedly when the boys rushed out of the car to meet him. He danced around, his thick tail beating the air, his wet tongue reaching for hands, faces, anything he could reach.

Ringo laughed uproariously when Susan leaned down with him so that he could pet the dog. Burgie kissed his tiny hands, then swept Susan's face with his large wet tongue.

Before Susan could issue a "not in your good jackets" warning, the boys were wrestling with Burgie on the lawn.

"Well!" a female voice said. "I'm the one who's come to help out and no one seems to notice me."

Susan turned to see the woman from the porch watching the boys with and indulgent smile.

Aaron wrapped her in a hug. "Hi, Beebee," he said. "What a nice surprise. What do you mean you've come to help out?"

"Well," she said, taking Ringo from Susan. "Four little boys, two working people. That doesn't sound like an equation that leaves much time for fun for anyone." Then she smiled down at the tangle on the grass. "Although children always do seem to manage, don't they?" She focused her attention on the boy in her arms. "This must be Ringo. There's a picture of you and your brothers on the refrigerator at home, you know," she said to the child.

Ringo studied her face, a puzzled frown on his brows. Then he put a hand to her nose and pulled.

"No, sweetie." Susan drew his hand away and smiled apologetically. "Sorry about that. I'm Susan Turner. Welcome to Princeton. How nice of you to…to…"

"Barge in?" Beebee caught Ringo's hand when he was about to try the nose trick again. "I do that. I'm sorry. I should have called, but then Aaron would have told me not to come, and that would have been no fun for any of us. This way, I don't have to try to keep busy in that big old lonely house. I can pack lunches, get the boys off to school, prepare meals, keep the house up—and the two of you can have a life."

"That's thoughtful, Beebee," Aaron said, "but in three weeks, I'm going home."

Beebee smiled. "Well, if I like it better here, I might just stay with Susan. Take me to the kitchen. I need coffee and I should check to see what we have for dinner." She looked over her shoulder at the boys in the grass, the dog leaping back and forth over them. "Boys, come along. You have to show me your rooms and what I can and cannot clean."

Fifteen minutes later a fresh pot of coffee was brewing, Beebee was planning on roast beef and vegetables for dinner, and the boys had taken her upstairs to show her their rooms, their expressions stunned.

"This is very thoughtful of her," Susan said, taking down cups, "and it's wonderful for you that she's obviously so devoted to you, but *where* are we going to put her?"

"That's easy." Aaron reached for the box of Twinkies and carried it to the table. Burgie danced around his feet, partly in adoration, partly in response to the smell of something sweet. "I'll move into your room and she can have mine."

Susan gave him a dirty look, took the Twinkie box from him and put it back on the shelf. She reached into the built-in cooler for an apple, then tossed it to Aaron. Burgie looked disappointed.

"You just had two doughnuts," Susan criticized. "You don't need more sugar." Then realizing he might interpret the "sugar" to mean his offer to move in with her, she dared him with a look to say it.

He grinned. "I thought it was a resourceful idea. At the Daddy Club meeting, Graber told us that we should always be looking for ways to help our kids, to make their lives easier, less stressful. I'm sure that extends to the women in our lives, also. Do you mind Burgie being in the house?"

"Of course not." Susan went back to the cooler for an orange. "I am not in your life," she said, sitting at the table to peel the fruit. The citrus smell rose immediately to combine with the flower fragrance she wore. The two filled his mind with thoughts of her in a sarong in the tropics.

He forced himself back to her argument as he took a seat at the table. ''That's right,'' he said, biting and chewing a chunk of apple. It was crisp and sweet. He offered a bite to Burgie, who turned up his nose and lay down at Aaron's feet. ''You've opted to ignore your feelings.''

''In the interest of the boys.''

He bounced a doubtful glance off her. ''Really. I wonder.''

She stopped peeling the orange and challenged him with a look. ''What does *that* mean?''

''That I think you're protecting yourself and not them,'' he said mercilessly.

''Has it occurred to you,'' she asked directly, ''that in putting your business above your personal life, you're doing the same thing?''

He considered denying that, then decided it would serve no purpose. She cared about him; she could see into him. Just as he could see into her.

''Yes, it has,'' he admitted. ''My stepmother had no use for Dave and me when our father died, and for the brief time we stayed with her, she did her best to make us feel small and worthless. Dave retreated to his music, and I hid out with the computers at school. Thanks to a sympathetic teacher, I learned that I did have a brain, that I could contribute.''

Susan's eyes widened and she leaned back in her chair. ''Becky told me you'd been emancipated at almost sixteen, but I didn't—''

''Freedom from Helen was a great relief. Dave was traveling with a band and I lived with friends. My teacher got me a scholarship to Princeton so I wouldn't have to worry about board, and found me a job to help pay my other expenses. I started the business right after college. It took a while to take off, but when it did, I felt powerful for the first time in my life. It was built out of all the agonies of those years and the underlying determination to prove Helen wrong.''

Usually he resisted telling the story. It made him feel vulnerable and he hated that. But this time he found freedom in it, a lightening of his spirit.

"So it's become everything to you," Susan said quietly. "The symbol of your worth as a human being."

"Yes."

She nodded as though she understood. "That's what the boys mean to me I guess. My family was sort of sad and disconnected, and I've always wanted a functional family more than I've ever wanted anything. So I can understand what drives you, but wouldn't it be healthier if your reason for living was people, instead of things?"

He spread his arms to indicate his surroundings. "I'm here and doing my best. But success is so much easier to determine with things than it is with people." He grinned. "If I was a product and you were a focus group, your reaction would convince me that I wasn't worth getting to the consumer."

"Then why do you persist?" she asked.

"Personal marketing research," he replied. "Your kiss canceled all your arguments on why we wouldn't work."

"I said—"

"I heard you. But what your heart wants is harder

to ignore than what your head wants. And someday you're going to change your mind."

Beebee came back downstairs with Ringo in her arms, his brothers behind her.

It had been hard enough to complete an argument with Susan with the boys almost always around, but it was going to be impossible with Beebee around, too.

"Beebee, come and sit down. You're probably exhausted after that long flight. You must have taken the red-eye."

Aaron stood to pull out a chair for her.

"Thank you." Beebee sat, and Ringo yawned sleepily. "It's very sweet of you to fuss over me, but I came to fuss over *you*. What if I just take over cooking and housekeeping duties while I'm here? And I can look after the boys when you have things to do."

John leaned a forearm on Aaron's shoulder when Aaron resumed his chair. "Beebee knows all about computers," he said in some surprise. "She says you taught her."

Aaron nodded. "Everything she knows," he boasted.

"And she's been to Africa!" Paul said, clearly impressed.

"My parents were anthropologists," she explained to Susan. "I lived there until I was twelve, then they sent me back to the States for school."

The boys seemed enthralled with Beebee. Susan tried to relax and think of her presence here as a good thing. At first she'd feared that she'd simply be someone else on Aaron's side, but he was as surprised by the woman's arrival as she was, and despite Beebee's take-charge attitude, she seemed warm and open.

"Why don't you change your clothes," Susan suggested to the boys, "and you can play ball while it's sunny. It's supposed to rain tomorrow."

John made a face as he walked desultorily toward the stairs. "We have to go to school tomorrow."

"I'll make apple pie while you're gone," Beebee promised "and when you get home, we'll celebrate your new adventure."

Paul, following John, turned to her, his eyes wide. "You can make pie?"

"Sure."

"Susan doesn't know how."

Beebee turned to Susan, who shrugged guiltily. "Well, I don't know how to build anything," Beebee said. "We all have our talents."

The boys hurried upstairs, cheered by the prospect of homemade pie. Several moments later they were changed into play clothes and their old jackets, and carrying their baseball gear.

"Can Burgie come with us?" John asked.

"Sure." Aaron pushed open the double door for them. "Just make sure you stay in the yard. If the ball goes in the road, what do you do?"

"Look both ways before going to get it," Paul replied.

"Good."

Susan took Ringo from Beebee. He was now rubbing his eyes and struggling to keep them open. "Why don't you spend the afternoon settling in," Susan suggested to Aaron's housekeeper, "and let me worry about dinner. Then tomorrow you can—"

"Nope." Beebee got to her feet. "Aaron will carry my bag up, won't you, dear?" she asked.

He looked away from the French doors through which he watched the children and nodded. "Of course, Oh Great One. I am yours to command."

She made a wry face at Susan. "He's a bit of a smart a—"

"Tell me about it," Susan replied, rocking Ringo.

Beebee seemed to like that reply. "Anyway, I'll get to work on finding things if you don't mind me rummaging around, then I'll see to dinner." She patted Susan's free shoulder. "You have the afternoon off, young lady. At least as long as Ringo naps."

Susan carried Ringo upstairs to his crib, changed the bedding in Aaron's room for Beebee, then put it in the washer so that she would have something for Aaron to use on the sofa bed.

Then she went back downstairs to see how the boys were doing.

"They're fine," Aaron assured her. He sat on the soft blue-and-gray plaid sofa in the living-room window that looked out onto the backyard, the newspaper spread out around him. "I've got an eye on them. The neighbor boys are here, too, and brought a couple of friends. There's a major-league team in development here."

She caught a whiff of something sweet and gingery. "What's that?" she asked.

"Beebee's making snickerdoodles. She promised me more coffee and a few cookies when they're ready."

Susan picked up a pile of papers and sat down, looking through them for the Sunday supplement.

"You should be taking a nap or something," he said.

"Yeah, right. So you don't have to share the cookies. I'm not sleepy."

Susan got comfortable in the middle of the sofa, the sunshine on her back, the aroma of cookies in the oven wafting around her. She opened the supplement to an article on salary comparisons in America.

She learned that buyers in small shops made nothing, that CEOs of major companies got bonuses that were more than she'd see in three lifetimes, and that a quiet hour with the sun on your back in the middle of a comfortable sofa could make a liar out of someone who'd claimed not to be sleepy.

She closed her eyes and drifted off into the most blissful space of warmth and comfort. She felt herself lean sideways, exploring the boundaries of her bed, and a sturdy bar seemed to go up, just as she lost that sense of solidity under her, in danger of falling off into the darkness. She was urged back to that warm embrace of space by a strong touch. A soft velvet rest claimed her.

SHE OPENED HER EYES to stock-market figures. Something called SorpLab was up two and a half points, and BrassIntl was down half.

She blinked. Then she realized she was sprawled atop something—a long and muscular...mattress? It seemed to be wearing a blue sweater and holding up the financial page.

She sat up abruptly and collided with something at the same moment that Aaron also moved and shouted a warning. Warm liquid fell onto her head and dripped through her hair, down her face, onto her sweater and onto Aaron's. Apparently his left hand, which was holding the paper, had also held a cup of coffee.

He tossed the paper aside and dabbed at her face with a napkin from the coffee table. "You okay?" he asked urgently. "Did it burn you?"

"No," she denied, confused and embarrassed. She pushed back a damp hank of hair that smelled of coffee. Her bangs were soaked, as was the front of her sweater. She frowned at Aaron. "What am I doing here?"

He arched an eyebrow, obviously surprised by the question. "You belong here," he replied.

She eyed him impatiently. "I mean, in your arms."

He gave one emphatic nod. "You belong here."

She pushed against him to sit up.

"Okay, okay," he said with a small laugh. "I noticed you had trouble keeping your eyes open. After a few minutes the magazine section went slack in your hands and you started to slip sideways. I happened to be in the way. I'm sorry. I thought the gentlemanly thing to do was to let you lean on me rather than shove you in the other direction." He plucked at the damp front of his sweater in good-humored distress. "But I got soaked in the process, and you don't seem to appreciate my chivalry."

She did appreciate it, but if she admitted it, they'd have that argument again. She didn't feel sufficiently clearheaded to maintain her end of it.

"At least the coffee missed the sofa," she said, standing up and examining the upholstery. "I'm sorry about your sweater. I'll put it in the wash for you and get you more coffee.''

He smiled up at her, one leg stretched out on the sofa, the other braced on the carpet. She'd been lying on that leg, she realized, and it had felt wonderful.

Though it couldn't have been that comfortable for him.

''You think doing those little things for me,'' he asked audaciously, ''will make up for what you really want to do for me?''

She shouldn't ask the question, she knew. She was playing into his hands.

But he had an appeal for her that was growing with each passing day, becoming bigger and more demanding than anything she'd ever experienced.

''What do I really want to do?'' she asked, pretending skepticism.

He looked into her eyes as though trying to reassure himself that what he thought she wanted was really there. She saw the flare in his eyes when he found it.

''You want to come back into my arms,'' he said quietly. ''You want to kiss me.''

Well. He was right about that. But she was smart enough to know that what she wanted posed a danger to her peace of mind. She took a step away from the sofa, intending to walk away, to do something practical and sense-restoring like taking the sheets out of the washer and putting them into the dryer.

But for the first time in ages, she didn't care about sense. And that was worrisome, because now she had four children to think about.

But this moment seemed to exist out of the time of

her real life. It was a little fantasy she could indulge in for ten seconds, maybe twenty. Maybe even get it out of her system so that it wouldn't haunt her every day—the very thing she'd always wanted dangling just beyond her reach.

He held out a hand to her but didn't touch her. He simply offered it—the way back to him if she dared take it.

She did.

She put her hand in his, but he remained still, letting her approach him.

She put one knee on the sofa, put her free hand on his shoulder and relaxed a little when she encountered that familiar warmth and strength. She smiled hesitantly as danger receded and indulgence beckoned.

He smiled in return, freed her hand to put both of his to her waist and guide her down to lie along the length of him until they were body to body, mouth to mouth.

One arm came around her to hold her to him while the other tangled in her hair. He watched her lower her mouth to his.

She felt a flash of excitement at being in charge of this. For a woman who felt as though she'd completely lost control of her life, it was heady stuff.

But she'd lost the will to be cautious. She was taking this moment and she wanted to be able to remember it.

She opened her mouth over his and took it with shameless desire. She dipped her tongue inside, explored, teased, sparred, her fervor ignited further by his enthusiastic response.

She wound her fingers in his hair, kissed him from

his hairline to his throat, while her heart thudded and a warm languor pooled deep inside her. A spicy fragrance clung to his skin and seemed to fill her awareness, to draw her down into its warm invitation and close over her head.

She came up gasping, flung out of the fantasy she'd thought this to be and accepting it for what it was—her reality.

GOOD GOD, AARON THOUGHT. *What have I done?* She was so pretty, so warm, so selflessly willing to do what she had to do for four little boys he loved very much, that letting himself flirt with falling in love with her had been a delicious indulgence. Making her confront what he was sure she felt for him had been a way of leveling the playing field, because he really was smitten.

But now that he'd let her take control of this encounter to clarify for both of them precisely where they stood, he realized what a stupid and insipid word ''smitten'' really was.

His body roared with feeling, screamed with impatience to know all of her, raged with the need to take her to his bed and show her what he knew they could do together.

To make her see that she had to come home with him.

But she had both hands braced on his shoulders, and she was looking down at him as though he'd somehow tricked her.

''That's...'' she whispered tremulously, ''that's real.''

Yes. He'd just come to understand that. This was

no game, no flirtation, and no fantasy to play with for the space of time they had.

This was a union of bodies and souls that wasn't going to take no for and answer.

"I told you," he said, letting himself feel superior for a moment to avoid allowing her to have the upper hand. Because if she got it, he'd walk away from everything to be with her and the boys—and he couldn't.

He couldn't, or he wouldn't be himself anymore.

But if she could come to him...

That gauzy thought was snatched away from him when she pushed herself to her feet and ran across the living room and up the stairs as though she couldn't escape him fast enough.

"I HOPE YOU UNDERSTAND why I came," Beebee said.

Aaron made his bed on the family-room sofa, Burgie wandering around the bed and whining, probably wondering where the stadium blanket was that he always slept on at the foot of Aaron's king-size bed in Seattle. His housekeeper appeared with two extra blankets. "Susan asked me to give you these."

Susan had avoided him since the incident on the living-room sofa that afternoon. She'd been subtle and he didn't think anyone had noticed, but it was clear it had unsettled her as much as it had him.

"I understand," he said, tossing the blanket onto the bed. "You've made it your life's work to meddle into mine. And when you heard there were children here, you had to come and spoil them."

She acknowledged that assessment with a nod.

"My grandchildren are in Texas, and you wouldn't give me any honorary ones in Seattle." She smiled maternally. "These little guys are adorable."

"Yeah." Agreeing with that was easy.

"It's going to be hard for you to leave them."

"Yes." He wasn't about to discuss this with her. He couldn't explain what he couldn't understand himself.

"And her, too?"

He was avoiding that one like an open manhole. He made a production of spreading blankets. "I told you she wasn't my type."

"I remember that," she said, catching the edge of the blanket on her side and smoothing it in place. She made an expert hospital corner. "But I saw you kiss her in a way they don't even allow on cable."

He looked up at her in disgruntled exasperation.

"What?" she asked defensively. "I'd promised you more cookies and I was trying to deliver them. I hadn't intended to snoop." He unfolded the second blanket and she caught it, easing it into place. "I just wanted to make sure you knew that that kind of passion doesn't come to everyone. And that when children bring you together, you're doubly blessed."

She walked around the bed to kiss his cheek. "I wanted to be here to help you," she said, giving his shoulders a squeeze. "Because I know this will be tough for you if you stay and tough on you if you go. I wanted you to know that I'm not just a fair-weather friend."

She'd already proved that many times—when he brought armies of staff home without warning for days at a time to solve programming problems that refused to be solved at the office, when reporters accosted her in the supermarket trying to find out about his latest product, when pipes burst in an upstairs bathroom while he was at a conference in France and she'd had to cope alone.

He hugged her tightly. She'd been the mother he could barely remember, the friend he never had time for, the staffer who was on twenty-four-hour call.

"Thanks, Beebee. I appreciate you, I really do. It'll help Susan a lot to have you around. And it's always a comfort to me to know you're there."

"Just remember," she said, walking toward the door, "that you're a genius. Everyone says so."

He knew better, but it helped business to let everyone think so. "And how does that help me here?"

"You've found solutions to problems in Starscape that everyone was sure didn't exist." She blew him a kiss. "You can do this."

Yeah.

He walked out into the backyard with Burgie, beyond where the children played ball, and leaned against a cedar tree while the dog sniffed around for his comfort spot.

He appreciated Beebee's faith in him. But Susan wasn't software.

Although...

Chapter Eight

John and Paul looked so frightened as Susan and Aaron waited with them in the principal's office of Stony Elementary that Susan would have happily taken them home with her for one more day and brought them back tomorrow. Rain fell in torrents beyond the office's big windows and contributed, she was sure, to the boys' gloomy expressions.

But they would still look like this tomorrow, she told herself firmly. Just as she might stand beside Aaron today and pretend that he didn't know she was in love with him, and that she didn't know he was in love with her. But there was no escaping that truth.

John's anguish turned to a smile when the boy sent by the third-grade teacher to take him to class was Stewie Marshall, one of the kids who made up their backyard baseball team.

A contingent of three children, two of them girls, came from the first-grade class to take Paul in. He looked the girls over, then turned worriedly to Aaron.

Aaron patted his shoulder. "You'll be fine. I'll pick you up after school."

"Okay." He did not sound at all convinced.

Susan and Aaron hurried back to the car, with him holding the wing of his raincoat over her. He took her to the passenger side rather than the driver's and snatched the keys from her hand.

"Hey!" she protested halfheartedly.

"What's your favourite color?" Aaron asked without preamble as he unlocked her door and helped her inside.

"Why?" she asked worriedly when he climbed in behind the wheel.

"Because I'm going to buy you something." He turned the key in the ignition, then headed for the exit to the street.

"Beebee's alone with George and Ringo," she reminded him.

"And up to the job." He pulled out into traffic and turned in the opposite direction from home. "I told her we'd be out until after lunch, and she said she was happy to be rid of us."

"Us?"

"Okay, me. Color?"

She resigned herself to some mysterious shopping expedition. In truth she loved the thought of a little time spent alone with him. Now into her second week in his company, she was able to admit, at least to herself, that she was falling in love. And grew more and more conscious that in no time at all, he'd be gone.

"All right." She relaxed in her seat, enjoying the intimacy of their confinement in the car while rain pounded on the roof and the windows and made the windshield wipers work hard. "Ruby and emerald have always been my favourite colors," she teased, "and if there's a diamond or two between them, so much the better."

"All right. Ruby and emerald."

She closed her eyes, enjoying the blissful if temporary freedom from children. "Wake me when we get to Tiffany's."

"No time for napping," he said. "We're here."

She felt the car make an abrupt turn and opened her eyes to see that they were not shopping for jewelry. He'd pulled into an automobile dealership.

She was speechless while he drove slowly down the long lineup of rain-spattered new cars until he reached the vans, then he barely crept along as he peered out the window.

"Aaron, what are you doing?" she demanded.

"I'm van shopping," he replied as they passed the different models.

"Oh, no, you don't." She glowered at him, but he didn't notice. He'd pulled to a stop to study an Expedition with a roof rack. She tugged the sleeve of his raincoat, forcing him to look at her. "I'm talking to you!"

He met her angry gaze with an expression that told her it didn't impress him. "I admire that you deal with the boys without shouting," he said mildly. "I'd appreciate it if you'd deal with me in the same way."

She dropped her hand in exasperation. "I apologize for shouting. But you are *not* buying me a car."

"One more year," he said, pointing with his thumb to the rear seat, "and the boys won't fit comfortably back there. I'm buying this for them."

"Then it'll sit in the garage until John is sixteen."

He shook his head impatiently. "That's selfish of

you. You'd rather they were sitting on top of each other because you have some perverse sense of pride?''

''You have a perverse sense of duty,'' she growled, ''but I'm not going to argue this with you again.''

''Thank you,'' he said, finding a place to park at the end of the lot.

By the time he ran around the car to open Susan's door, a salesman appeared, standing under a large red golf umbrella.

''May I help you?'' he offered, holding the umbrella over Aaron.

''We're looking at vans,'' Aaron said. He offered his hand to Susan. When she ignored it, he smiled apologetically at the salesman. ''We're not entirely in agreement about this.''

''Well, someone in the family has to keep an eye on the bottom line,'' the salesman said philosophically—and a little patronizingly. ''But you won't know if what we have to offer is worth endangering the budget unless you take a look.''

The salesman had no idea that Aaron could probably buy the entire dealership and not even notice it, but she had to admire his attempt to do his job even with what he considered a recalcitrant wife in the way. And he hadn't just stepped over her; he was trying to work with her. He should get points for that.

She swung her legs out of the car and leaned into the umbrella's wide field of protection.

Aaron put an arm around her shoulders to make movement easier as the salesman conscientiously tried to keep them dry.

"I'm Larry, by the way," the salesman said, shaking hands with Aaron, then with Susan.

"She'll be ferrying four little boys," Aaron said as they stopped in front of the Expedition. "One of them is still in a child seat. And she needs some hauling room."

"Antique shopper?" the salesman asked genially.

"Carpenter," she replied.

His forehead wrinkled. "Really?" The man's eyes narrowed, then widened, and he grinned from ear to ear. "You're that little thing the guys in the body shop love to watch! You have a show for women on doing their own building and repairs. Last week you put a new front on a fireplace."

"That's right." She was flattered, but still too annoyed with Aaron to let him think she was glad she'd gotten out of the car. "You watched?"

"We all did."

"You have a fireplace?"

"No."

"One of the other men does?"

"No. We just like to watch because—" He stopped. "You're always so…" He stopped again.

Susan was beginning to understand. "You were making fun of a woman doing a man's job, weren't you? Maybe even hoping I'd make a mistake, maybe router my finger off?"

The salesman was clearly surprised by that question and flushed as he obviously decided his explanation for his stammering might be more acceptable than her deduction.

"We like you in you coveralls," he said bravely, sliding Aaron a sheepish smile of apology. Then realizing that he'd probably jeopardized the sale, he asked, "Would you like me to get you another salesman?"

Aaron bit back a smile but let Susan make the decision.

"You'll be fine," she said, then pointed at Aaron. "He's the one buying the car. But the next time you watch, I'd appreciate it if you did it with the intention of learning something."

He nodded, mortified. "I will."

The deal was made in an hour with the trade-in of her compact. Aaron decided on the Expedition because of its size and construction, because it already had a roof rack for the hauling she did so much of, and because it was green—one of her jewel color choices.

Larry was wide-eyed and a little skeptical when Aaron wrote a check for the full amount—three times what Susan had paid for her car. "Hold on while I get your receipt," he said disappearing into an office and closing the door.

Aaron and Susan sat in the showroom waiting area on a red leather seat that looked as though it had been taken out of a Volkswagen bus.

"You have to drive home," Aaron said flipping through a copy of *Newsweek*.

"It's your car," she said stubbornly. "It's not *my* car."

"I have a headache," he said.

"Darn." She leaned back in the seat. "And I was going to seduce you tonight."

"Yeah, right. Kissing me makes you run in terror."

"Don't start with me."

"*You're* the one who started it."

When five minutes had passed without a sign of Larry, Susan leaned forward, her elbows on her knees. "Why does it take so long to get a receipt?"

"Because he's probably calling the bank." Aaron closed the magazine and tossed it on the table. "I wouldn't want an employee to take that big a check without making sure there were funds to cover it."

"True." She rested her chin in her hand and turned to him. "It isn't *always* fun to have so much money, is it? I'll bet a lot of the time people don't really believe you're you."

"That happens."

"And you probably have to have a security system."

"I do. But everyone should have one."

"So you're okay with it? Being rich?"

"Usually. Sometimes—when people fear you or avoid you because they're sure you have to be different or cruel—then it's a problem. But most of the time it's a kick to buy what you want or go where you want to."

That did sound like fun, and despite their disagreement over the car and his extravagances with the children, she thought he was probably one of the most unpretentious men she'd ever met.

Bossy, maybe, but unpretentious.

"Have you ever gone to Paris for lunch?"

"No. Lindsey's on Cape Cod, though, for fried clams."

"I love those."

He smiled at her, rubbing a hand gently between

her shoulder blades. "Then it's a date. Before I leave, we'll go to Lindsey's."

Larry returned with a receipt and the now-familiar look of mortification. "*The* Aaron Bradley!" he said, taking the umbrella and walking them out to the lot. "I'm sorry I didn't recognize the name."

"You did recognize Susan," Aaron teased. "It's just that I don't look as good in coveralls."

Larry held the umbrella over them as they transferred Susan's tool kit and a few other things she kept in the trunk to the van. She emptied the glove box, took the document wallet she kept on the visor, then the maps from the door pockets.

Everything she needed retrieved, she simply stared at her little car a bit sad that she'd never see it again. Then she braced herself with the insight that the little car went with her old little life. Her *new* life required four-wheel drive, the tow package, and satellite positioning.

Aaron handed her the keys and walked around to the passenger door. "What do you want to do for lunch?"

She climbed in behind the wheel and buckled her belt.

"Something," he continued, as he climbed in beside her, "we don't have to eat with a napkin wrapped around it and a squeeze packet of ketchup."

"There's a small restaurant on Nassau Street that has wonderful food. They have the best pan-fried oysters in the entire world."

"All right. Let's go."

THE PLACE WAS PERFECT for a rainy-day rendezvous, Aaron thought. The dining room was painted white with dark wood trim. It was decorated with blue and yellow dried hydrangea arranged in Chinese-porcelain vases, two on a plain board mantel and half a dozen more placed about the room.

Watery daylight lent a soft atmosphere and an easy intimacy to their early lunch of oysters.

"Can you at least claim the van as a business expense?" Susan asked as she speared a baby carrot with her fork. She now seemed resigned about the van.

He shook his head. "I never try to deceive the IRS. I'm sure they look me over with a magnifying glass."

"One of the not-fun parts of being rich."

"Definitely."

"Well, thank you." She ate a bite of the carrot, then moved the other half around with the tip of her fork. She looked up at him suddenly, her eyes turbulent and wistful. "Life with the boys will be much easier because you've been so generous."

"They're my nephews," he said.

"I know. But their care was given to me. You could have let it go at that."

Now he was confused. She'd taunted him more than once because he hadn't spent enough time with his family. Now she was suggesting he could have just left her in charge and walked away?

"No, I couldn't have." He buttered a slice of hot French bread and put it on her bread plate. "And how come you're saying nice things to me? Is this part of that seduction you told me you had planned?"

She laughed lightly, tossing her hair back and wrinkling her nose. He found both gestures heartbreakingly endearing. "You have a headache, remember?" she said.

"It's gone. A miracle."

A frown replaced her smile. "I just don't think we should spend our time together fighting. We want happy memories of each other, don't we?"

Before he could assure her that he already had many—and that he was determined to have many more—she said briskly, "Eat up. I have to make plans this afternoon for what I want Flynn O'Grady to do with the addition."

The cell phone he'd placed beside his coffee cup rang. He sent Susan an apologetic smile.

"Hello?"

"Aaron?" It was Beebee.

She never bothered him unless she had a problem she couldn't handle. And she could usually handle anything. He experienced a mild prickle of panic.

"Something wrong with George or Ringo?"

Susan dropped her fork and stared at him, a frown pleating her forehead.

"Not with the little ones," she said, sounding anxious, "but the principal of the school called. Seems John and Paul have gotten into a fight."

"What?" he couldn't believe it. "They don't even know anybody to fight with yet."

"Apparently they do. John broke the other boy's Ascentilator."

Aaron spent frantic moments trying to recall what part of the anatomy that was until Beebee explained, "It's apparently some kind of flying-action-figure thing. The boys are pretty upset, so the principal thought it would be a good idea if you picked them up.''

Aaron explained the call to Susan as he closed the phone. He was about to ask her if she wanted him to have the waitress pack up their lunches, but she was already on her way out the door.

Aaron left cash, afraid that if he took the time to pay with a credit card she'd drive off without him.

IT LOOKED AS THOUGH it had been more of a wrestling match than a fight. Their clothes were smudged, but there didn't seem to be any bruises on John or Paul.

The other boy, red-haired and bigger than John but in his class, was just as disheveled. His mother held him protectively in front of her, her hands crossed over his chest.

Susan looked the boys over, then, certain they weren't seriously hurt, she put a hand on each boy's shoulder. ''What happened?'' she asked.

''They attacked my son, that's what happened,'' the redhead's mother replied, tightening her grip on her boy.

Aaron was astonished when Susan spun on her, both hands held protectively in front of *her* boys. He half expected to see her hair stand on end and a growl issue from her throat.

But she spoke quietly. ''These are two very peaceful children,'' she said breathlessly. ''And this is their first day in this school. If they attacked your son, I'm sure they were provoked.''

''He called us orphans!'' John said, tears welling in his eyes. He squared his shoulders and sniffed rather than let them fall.

Aaron hadn't felt quite that same pain as a child, but he'd hurt enough to understand the need to make sure no one else knew. Or to at least think they didn't.

"You are!" the redhead shouted back. "Your mother's dead and your father's dead! That makes you orphans!"

The boy's mother turned her son around and looked at him with sudden displeasure. "James Brooks! What a terrible thing to say!"

"But it's true!" the boy insisted. "They're orphans!"

"I'm sorry." The principal, Mrs. Harris, a thirtyish woman in a long denim dress and eyeglasses, looked very apologetic. "We always tell the teachers everything we can about new children, so they'll be able to help them deal with their new surroundings. I think perhaps James overheard our discussion."

"We are not orphans!" John raged, grabbing Susan's arm with a ferocity that startled her. "This is my mom now." Then he reached for Aaron's coat sleeve and yanked him closer. "And this is my dad! He used to be my uncle, but he's moved in with us and now he's my dad! Our parents died, but we got another set!"

Susan looked up at Aaron, at a loss to know what to do.

"You apologize this instant!" James Brooks's mother insisted.

"But why couldn't I say it?" James wanted to know. "It's true."

"You hate it when Grandma calls you carrottop, don't you? And that's true. It's never right to be hurtful, even if what you say is the truth."

"It *isn't* true," Paul grumbled.

Aaron put a hand on his shoulder to silence him.

James's mother pushed her son closer to John and Paul. "Apologize, or no Pirate Prince for a week!"

James folded his arms. "I'm sorry!" he shouted. "And who cares about Pirate Prince? You never got me the Island Treasure disk, anyway."

"I couldn't find it," Mrs. Brooks said, "and that's not the issue here, James!"

"John and Paul have the Island Treasure disk," Aaron said. "I'll bet they could make you a copy just to prove they're sorry, too. Right guys?"

John met Aaron's eyes with a look that said as clearly as words, *No way!*

Paul, however, never one to hold a grudge, said, "I could. If I knew how to make copies."

"I'll help you," Aaron promised. "John?"

"I'm not an orphan," John said, his arms folded and his mouth pinched as he stared across the room.

"James understands that now," Mrs. Brooks said. "But it's illegal to make copies, isn't it? And I…"

Aaron nodded, smiling. "Not if you're the man who created the game."

The woman gasped. James stared openmouthed. John and Paul looked vindicated.

Susan was surprised. "I thought you created business software?"

Aaron shrugged. "It just sort of came to me one day and it worked. So we marketed it. We'd be happy to provide James with it," Aaron said to James's mother.

"Well—" Mrs. Brooks returned his smile "—if your boys would be nice enough to make him a copy of Island Treasure, then I'll take them all skating and out for ice cream after it's installed.''

John's mercenary soul came to the fore. ''Okay,'' he said, ''but I want to hear him say it one more time.''

James, as though that was now all secondary to the new plan negotiated by the grown-ups, said, ''Okay, okay. You're not an orphan. I didn't know about the new parents.''

The principal breathed a sigh of relief. ''Now that's what we like to see,'' she said. ''Everybody helping out to make things work. I think you should all go home, get cleaned up and rested, and we'll start fresh tomorrow, okay?''

''Who does this belong to?'' John asked when Aaron and Susan led the boys out to the big green van.

''Us,'' Susan said unlocking it with the remote. ''Your uncle bought it for us.''

''He's my dad,'' John said, willing her with his eyes to agree.

''John—''

''He's my dad. For now.''

Aaron smiled inwardly at the boy's bargaining skills. When you can't get the opposition to agree, work the plan until you can. He'd bought and sold competitors himself on just the same principle.

They sat in the van for several minutes, giving the boys time to look it over and try everything that could be tested.

Susan put the key in the ignition.

''Okay, guys,'' Aaron said. ''Let's see how the seat belts work.''

BEEBEE FUSSED OVER THE BOYS, helped Susan get them bathed and changed, then went back downstairs to start dinner while Aaron watched afternoon cartoons with George, Ringo and Burgie.

Changed into play clothes, John went to his computer while Paul played on the floor with his trucks.

Susan was considering how best to approach the matter of John's insistence that Aaron was his new father when the boy seemed to read her mind and announced in an aggressive tone, "Uncle Aaron *has* to be our new dad."

Handed her opening, Susan searched an instant too long for the right words.

"Because you're our new mom and we saw you."

"Saw me?"

"Uncle Aaron and you," John answered, turning on his monitor and his computer. "Kissing like a mom and dad."

Oh, boy. "Sometimes adults kiss," Susan said, "because they're getting to know each other."

Paul looked up from his trucks. "I thought kissing came *after* you know somebody."

That should be true; usually it was true with her. But either she'd gotten to know Aaron Bradley very quickly, or this need she had to be near him outweighed her ability to understand him. Because she didn't.

"Sometimes…" Her voice cracked, so she cleared it and tried again. "Sometimes when adults hold and kiss each other," she said, "they learn things about each other that words don't say very well."

"Feelings?" John asked.

"Yes!" Susan patted his shoulder triumphantly.

"That's another reason I feel like he's my dad," John said. "When he plays with us and takes care of us—even when he tells us not to do something—he's just like my dad used to be. And he looks like him, kinda."

"But, John—"

"When we went to church," John went on, "you said we could leave our mom and dad a message. So I asked them to make Uncle Aaron our dad."

"We already got you," Paul said, "but *you* don't got anybody."

Susan knew when she was defeated. "I'll just go get you guys some hot cocoa." She retreated to the kitchen.

EVERYONE HAD GONE to bed and the house was quiet when Aaron climbed into his sofa bed and turned on Leno at half volume. Burgie climbed onto the foot of the bed and sprawled out on his stomach, his head on Aaron's ankles.

The monologue had barely begun when Susan appeared in the family-room door. She wore a burgundy velour robe with gold ribbon swirling along the hem and sleeves. It made the robe look like a royal garment, but he thought longingly of the brief nightshirt she probably wore underneath.

Burgie thumped his tail a time or two, then settled down again.

Aaron aimed the remote at the television and the room went silent.

"You *weren't* teasing about seduction?" he asked hopefully.

She came to sit on the corner of the bed opposite

Burgie. "John doesn't think we're teasing," she said seriously.

"About what?"

"He saw us kissing," she said. "That's why he's convinced you're their new dad. Because I'm their new mom and you were kissing me. I tried to explain that adults sometimes kiss to get to know each other, but he didn't buy it."

"Astute child."

She swatted his foot through the blanket. Burgie sat up, decided she did not pose a threat that required his defense and lay down again.

"Don't be smart," she scolded. "His second reason for believing it is that when we were in church on Sunday, he asked his mom and dad to make *you* their new dad."

He knew she was working around to blaming him for some of this, but he was definitely dodging this one. "Now that's your fault. You're the one who told them they could talk to God and their parents."

"I told him he could talk to God. Paul's the one who made the God-heaven-parents connection. But whoever's to blame, what do we do now? John's thinking of you as his father. And I have a feeling by the argumentative way he says it that somewhere deep down he knows it isn't true and he's just trying to comfort himself. The longer we let him do that without taking a stand against it, the harder it's going to be for him when you leave."

"Then maybe you'd better consider coming with me," he said.

"Aaron, this isn't funny!" Her voice rose. "I'm the

one who's going to have to cope with this when you're gone!''

"Then maybe," he repeated with quiet emphasis, "you should consider coming with me."

She shot to her feet and paced across the room, then turned on him, jabbing a finger into the air. "This is just like you. Spread your charm and your generosity but in the end make everyone do what you want them to do."

He sighed patiently. "Don't blame me for this. You care as much as I do about us—and them—but you're being just as inflexible."

She folded her arms. "Then maybe *you* should consider staying."

"That can't happen," he said firmly. "And aren't you trying to make everyone do what *you* want by insisting on that?"

"No." She came closer to the bed. "The boys and I already live here. You're the one who won't compromise."

"They've lived in this house all of a week," he argued. "If they want to be with me as much as you think they do, I'm sure they'd adjust to Seattle. And so would you."

She closed her eyes and tipped her head back as though summoning patience. He knew she'd also closed her mind.

"I'd appreciate it if you'd try to talk to him when you feel the time is right," she said. "Please try to make him understand."

"And how do I explain the kissing?"

She sighed. "Tell him we were getting to know

each other and decided we didn't like each other, after all. Good night, Aaron.''

She headed for the door.

He climbed out of bed and pushed the door closed before she could open it, crowding her against it with his body.

"That would mean lying to him," he said, the scent of her wafting around him, filling his senses.

"It's a white lie."

He turned her around so that she faced him. "It's a big fat black one and you know it."

She looked into his face, her eyes tired and grim. "Do you know how to explain to a child that two people can love each other and still choose not to be together?"

He studied her a moment, then pushed away, depressed to hear their situation distilled into that illogical sentence.

"No, I don't," he admitted.

She pulled the door open.

"Then lying's our best bet." And she was gone.

Chapter Nine

The rest of the week was uneventful. Susan checked daily with the school and learned that the boys seemed to be adjusting and were working well with their classmates.

Aaron copied the disk, picked up John, Paul and James after school on Thursday and took them to James's home to help them install the game, then left them in Mrs. Brooks's care.

She brought them home late that evening full of pizza, ice cream and cheerful camaraderie. All the boys glowed. "Thank you," Ginny Brooks said while the boys introduced James to Burgie, who appreciated the new arrival with leaps and barks and licks. "I'm grateful you chose to work this out with me when James was at fault. His father left us last year, and James tries to take it out on everyone. Anyway, I'm glad they're all friends now. It shows my son that people can disagree but still work out the problem without having to walk away like his father did."

Susan hugged her. "I'm glad it worked out, too. John and Paul need friends."

Beebee appeared between the two women, holding

a plastic-wrapped plate covered with pieces of the cobbler she'd baked for dessert. "I made too much," she said to Mrs. Brooks.

"How nice of you." Ginny gratefully accepted the plate. "I never have time to bake. Particularly now." She rolled her eyes. "I'm a tax accountant. Well, we'd better be on our way. Thanks again for the disk. The boys all had such a good time this afternoon."

Aaron nodded. "I'm glad."

Ginny called James. As they walked out to their car, James could be heard pleading for a puppy.

Susan closed the door, speculating about what had separated the Brookses. "She's so pretty," she said to Aaron, "and smart if she's a tax accountant. You'd think with a child in the picture the husband would have tried to work it out."

"Yes," Aaron said the tone of his voice underlining the words. "You'd think anyone would try a little harder at compromise when children are in the picture."

As she caught the implication in that, he hustled the boys upstairs to start their showers.

THE DADDY CLUB potluck offerings covered two large picnic tables in the park's community building, a log structure with kitchen facilities, picnic tables and old overstuffed furniture lining the walls. The park boasted a small lake and acres of grass and playground equipment.

As Susan pulled into the parking lot, she noticed women were few in number. Small crowds of men and children milled about, pulling covered dishes, bags of groceries, balls and games out of their cars.

John, Paul and George tried to run off the instant Susan opened the Expedition's doors.

"Hey!" Aaron shouted, stopping them in their tracks. Their attention captured, he turned to Susan. "Any last-minute instructions?"

"Stay together," she said. "No punching, biting, anything like that." She caught a glimpse of the beautiful sun-embroidered lake and added quickly, "And stay out of the water!"

They nodded and ran off toward the playground equipment, where all the other children were headed. Susan took Ringo out of his seat while Aaron let Beebee out the back.

"I'm not sure I've ever heard of a picnic in April," Beebee said, buttoning the top button of her jacket. She wore a small-brimmed denim hat, the front brim held up against the crown with a yellow silk flower.

"The dads in this group are always looking for ways to keep the kids happy," Aaron explained, opening the tailgate and handing her a wrapped plate of her famous deviled eggs. "And some of them live in apartments or condos, and the kids have grown stir-crazy over the winter. They thought this would be a way to help them blow off steam."

She tipped her chin in the direction of the children shrieking and laughing as they attacked the swings, slides and monkey bars. "It looks as though it's working already."

Susan frowned as she watched the boys blend into the crowd of other children. "I dressed them in the same color so we could keep track of them," she said worriedly. "Their old red jackets when they're outside, blue sweatshirts when we're inside. But I've already lost sight of them."

Aaron pulled out a paper bag filled with potato and tortilla chips. He took Ringo from Susan and handed her the bag.

"See the big guy going down the slide?" he asked.

She swung her gaze in that direction. "It's Micah," she said with a little laugh.

"The club's posted a list somewhere inside of rotating playground duty. A dad will be watching all the time. I'm two o'clock to three."

"I'm impressed." She hauled out a foil-wrapped pan of lasagna that Aaron balanced on the flat of one hand as she closed the tailgate. "That's very efficient."

"I think the chairman of this event is a schoolteacher. Conditioned to think of everything."

"What's he look like?" She followed Beebee, who'd headed off at a brisk pace toward the building.

Aaron formed the end of the parade, holding the pan out of Ringo's reach. "Why?"

"Just wondered," she replied with a brief glance over her shoulder. "Elaine and Darcie said they're working on getting the Daddy Club dads married off. And schoolteachers don't travel."

AARON IGNORED THE TAUNT and refused to let his mind stray to the thought of her glossy hair and her floral scent luring another man into discovering all her appealing qualities.

He felt as pugnaciously possessive about Susan as John felt about making him his father.

Ruth Naomi ran to greet them the moment they

walked through the door. "Hi guys! How's it all going? It's so good to see you." She paused to frown at the newcomer, as though a little concerned about competition for stand-in mom. "Hello," she said. "I'm Ruth Naomi Steadwell."

Beebee nodded, also a little stiffly, clearly recognizing an equal power. "Beulah Bernice Pottersby."

"Otherwise known as Beebee," Aaron put in, fascinated by this meeting. It reminded him of Godzilla meeting Mothra. He half expected lightning to strike, tides to surge, buildings to fall. "Beebee manages my house in Seattle. She came out to help Susan and me."

"Well." Ruth Naomi pointed toward the kitchen. "Just take your things in there. Let me have this little guy—" she took Ringo from Aaron's arms "—and I'll take him to the nursery we've set up for infants and toddlers. A couple of my friends are helping out."

Ringo went without protest, smiling as Beebee tickled his stomach.

Two dads in white aprons manned the kitchen, one forming burger patties, the second arranging what looked like Ruth Naomi's muffins on a tray.

Aaron recognized the hamburger dad as the group's president, about whose efficiency he'd just boasted to Susan.

To prove to himself that he could be bigger than his jealousy, he made introductions. He took her arm and led her to the counter where the man worked. "Susan, I'd like you to meet Darrell Dimitrio, chairman of the Daddy Club's potluck. Darrell, Susan Turner, new mom."

"Of course." Darrell wiped his hands on his apron, then extended one to her. "Aaron told us about you at the last meeting. He said he attended our meeting to hope to catch up with just a little bit of what you seemed to know instinctively about parenting."

Susan turned to Aaron in pleased surprise. "You did?"

Darrell reclaimed her attention. "He did. Ruth Naomi said she visited the other day and you have everything running smoothly."

"As smooth as life ever gets with four little boys."

Darrell took an apron from the folded stack beside him and handed it to her. "I could use some help with these burgers. Do you mind being conscripted?"

Maybe this was fate, she decided. Her emotions were snagged in a relationship that had taken her by storm but seemed to have no positive direction.

Maybe the practical thing to do was look in other directions. Her life was all about children now. There was something to be said for a man who worked normal hours, was home weekends, and who also always had to put children first.

"Ah...no." She unfolded the apron and tucked her head through the neck loop.

"Good." Darrell turned to smile in Aaron's direction. "I hope you don't mind, but I switched playground duty times with you so I could get the food ready. You're on now."

Aaron nodded, admiring Dimitrio's ploy to get Susan to himself.

"Sure." He tied Susan's apron strings, finding something significant in the gesture. "Anything you need before I go, Susan?"

She studied him, clearly a little uncertain what was going on. "No, I'm fine. Thank you. I'll save a place for you in line."

"Great."

Aaron went out to the playground to relieve Micah, but his friend seemed in no hurry to leave. An overgrown child himself, Micah watched the wild action of little bodies running, swinging, and moving hand over hand on the monkey bars with a smile on his face.

"Aren't they just amazing?" he said as Aaron stood beside him, assessing the situation, picking out the ones to watch: the towhead hanging by his knees from the monkey bars, the little girl on the middle swing pumping higher than the boys on either side of her, the long line forming on the slide as seven children planned to go down together—Paul and George among them.

Aaron scanned the play area and found John climbing a sugar maple with two other boys.

"Yes," he agreed, "they are. You considering having your own?"

Micah shrugged. "I don't know. The owner of a nightclub isn't the kind of dad you want to take to show-and-tell."

Aaron detected serious grimness in Micah's voice. "You're kidding right? I think kids would find the guy who hires bands and bouncers far more exciting than a programmer or a mailman."

Micah considered that moodily, then turned to him with a grin.

"How's it going at Susan's house? And how come

you're still here? I thought you were going home a week and a half ago?''

"I intended to," Aaron replied, trying to keep his eye on all the quickly moving little bodies, though his mind kept drifting to Susan. ''But I began to see that she couldn't be expected to do it all alone.''

"So you're staying?"

"For two more weeks."

Micah turned to him, narrowing one eye against the bright sun. ''And that's the magic time when she *will* be able to do it alone?''

"Hey." Aaron jammed his hands in his pocket and started to walk, needing desperately to move, to get his mind off Susan working shoulder to shoulder with Darrell Dimitrio, the nine-to-five man. ''I can't stay here. I'm caught in the Wall Street version of 'the show must go on.' You understand all about that. You do what you have to do because a million details that involve a lot of other people's livelihoods or money are tied to your performance.''

"Yeah." Micah followed him, sidetracking to catch a wayward ball and toss it back to the knot of little girls who'd lost it. ''And Starscape's been a part of you for such a long time. I remember the tour that took me to the Tacoma Dome and I stayed an extra night to have dinner with you and tour Starscape. I was pretty jaded from being on the road by then, and I thought it was cool that you were so energized by what you were doing.''

"I still am."

"But there's something between you and Susan, isn't there?"

"Yes."

"And she can't go with you?"

Aaron shook his head. "She has another year on her contract with the cable station. She says the kids have just been uprooted and made to readjust—they shouldn't have to do it again."

"That's a tough one. But the boys seem wild about you. Wouldn't it be worse to deprive them of you than to move them?"

Aaron sighed. "I don't know. Dave and Becky put the kids in Susan's care. It's her decision. And she's dealing with some baggage about her father, who was never around. She doesn't want the boys to have to deal with that, and you know how I work—long hours, lots of trips."

Micah nodded. "Isn't there a middle ground in there somewhere?"

That reminded Aaron of John's suggestion. "The kids want to move New Jersey closer to Washington."

"Well that's creative, but I was thinking along the lines of something more doable."

"Yeah. Right now I just don't know what that would be. Whoa!"

The seven children going down the slide together had added two more and were now a squirming tangle of arms and legs at the bottom.

Aaron and Micah ran to assess the damage. The loud laughter suggested it was minimal.

SUSAN COVERED THE TABLE next to the kitchen service window with paper cloth, then grouped the large pump dispensers of ketchup, mustard and mayonnaise on it, along with bowls of relish and chopped onions.

Paper plates and napkins had already been set out. Darrell peered through the service window at her. "A little closer to the middle," he said, "so that people can get to it from both sides. That's it."

Susan complied, then went back into the kitchen. Darrell held out a forkful of potato salad to her, his hand cupped under it. "Do you think this is salty enough?"

She took a bite. "I think it's fine."

His expression seemed to dispute that. "I think it needs a little something. Celery seed, maybe?"

She looked at him in surprise. "Does this kitchen even have celery seed?"

"I could run home."

"Darrell," she said practically, "I don't think the kids will notice the lack of celery seed."

"They might not," he agreed, helping himself to another taste from the large silver bowl. He closed his eyes, apparently analyzing. "But we're supposed to teach them a little style."

She thought about the boys gathered around her dinner table at home, and thought style was probably the last thing they cared about. Particularly on a picnic.

He put the bowl of potato salad back into the refrigerator, took off his apron and reached for his jacket. "And I'll bring some paprika for the deviled eggs," he said as he left.

Beebee, Susan knew, had deliberately left off the paprika because Aaron didn't like it, but Darrell was gone before she could say that. Ruth Naomi came into the kitchen to top off her cup of coffee. "How's it going?" she asked.

"Good," Susan reported.

"Where's Darrell?"

"He went home to get celery seed for the potato salad."

"What?" Ruth Naomi demanded. "That's *my* potato salad. My family likes it the way it is." She went to the refrigerator to pull it out. She took a fork from the drawer and tasted it. "There's nothing wrong with this."

Susan agreed. "I thought so, too. But Darrell says he's trying to teach the children a little style."

Ruth Naomi put the potato salad back, then dusted off her hands. "He's going to get a piece of my mind." The murder in her eye suggested he'd be lucky if that was all he got.

The other kitchen dad enlisted Susan to help grill the meat.

The aroma began to draw adults and children alike, and Susan didn't even surface from her chores until an hour later when everyone had been served and she went through the line herself.

Ruth Naomi must have missed Darrell's return to the kitchen, because Susan noticed the sprinkling of the tiny dark celery seeds through what was left of the potato salad, and paprika on the last remaining deviled egg.

She looked the room over to find her family and saw that the Steadwells had joined them, leaving no room at the table. Ruth Naomi and Beebee sat on one corner in earnest conversation.

Darrell, seated with a boy and a girl about eight or nine respectively on either side of him, and another family across the table, beckoned Susan to join them.

She looked longingly in the direction of her family's table, but went to sit next to Darrell's son.

Darrell introduced her to his children. She recognized the other father and his little girls from the meeting at Hardware and Muffins.

"Sit up straight, son," Darrell said to his boy. "You're getting that relish all over. Oh, now there you go, on your good jeans. That's going to need a stain-lifter."

Susan reached over with a napkin to try to help.

"Blot don't rub," Darrell advised.

Susan wondered if Darrell knew how close he was coming to wearing his food. And possibly a chair.

"What do you like best about school, Sean?" Susan asked, trying to relax what appeared to be a very tense little boy.

"I like history." Sean smiled up at Susan, clearly pleased with her interest. "You know why they called the Minutemen the Minutemen? Because they could be—"

"He's better in math." Darrell talked right over him. "We talked about that, Sean, remember? It's important to identify early what you're really good at and pursue that for the most efficient use of your skills. And let's face it, accountants make a lot more money than history teachers."

Susan stared at Darrell. "I'm a little surprised that you, as a teacher would take that attitude. Wouldn't someone be more inclined to excel at something he found fascinating? Wouldn't he want to learn more, work harder, make more of a contribution?"

Darrell stared at her. "Fascination doesn't sustain a career. Good income does."

"Then why are you teaching?"

"Because I sell Harway products on the side. I'd like to talk to you about that while we clear up the kitchen. You can become part of our magic future for a very small investment. We sell…"

Susan's eyes drifted longingly in the direction of her family's table. Conversation seemed to be lively, and she could hear the laughter above the drone of Darrell's voice.

The boys looked happy interspersed among the adults and included in the conversations. Ringo sat on Aaron's knee and helped himself to cut-up pieces of hamburger, fruit and the three-bean salad he seemed to be enjoying one bean a time.

She finally excused herself and hurried into the kitchen for respite. If she had to listen to Darrell one more minute, she'd be forced to run home for her rivet gun and seal his lips forever.

She poured herself a much-needed cup of coffee and leaned back against the stainless-steel sink to take a long deep sip.

Aaron walked into the kitchen carrying several empty bowls from the potluck table. Every nerve ending in her body came awake, and the edgy tension that had pressed down on her since she'd made the terrible mistake of getting better acquainted with Darrell evolved into something that made her feel as though her emotional gauge had risen into the red zone.

She straightened away from the counter, her body taking control of her brain and acting on its own.

AARON HAD NOTICED Susan's and Darrell's apparent interest in each other throughout lunch. She'd listened to him with such seriousness, and he'd seemed to go on and on as though he had so much to share.

It was selfish of Aaron to hate their appeal for each other. But it didn't look as though his relationship with Susan was going to go any farther, and the simple truth was she was going to need help with the boys—and from someone who wasn't three thousand miles away.

The best thing he could do was be supportive and live with his own disappointment.

"Hi." He put down the bowls and rolled up the sleeves of his navy-blue fleece shirt. "I thought you might want some help with—"

He wasn't sure what to make of it when she put down her cup and grabbed his shirtfront in a fist. Her eyes were dark and stormy, complicated emotions roiling in them. Anger. Confusion. Passion. Frustration.

She was pushing him backward, and he was too busy trying to understand what was going on to stop her.

She was angry at him, but it was a lot more than that. Her eyes were going over his face in a slow deliberation that made him uncertain whether to fear for his life or his virtue.

While he analyzed that, she backed him into the little square of space around the corner at the far end of the kitchen where a mop and a broom were propped up in a corner.

"How dare you?" she demanded, pushing him up against the wall.

"How dare I what?"

Something shifted in her eyes and all the conflicting feelings in them melded into one easily identifiable emotion.

Desire.

She rose up on tiptoe, looped her arm around his neck and, her body pressed to his from breast to knee, kissed him with all that pent-up passion.

It brought out everything he felt for her, all the love and affection he'd tried to put away when it seemed clear it had no place to go.

He wasn't sure it did now, but it was in play, anyway. It roared through him and he did his best to share it with her.

She leaned against him so completely as she kissed him that he was sure all that supported her were her arms around his neck. He helped with a hand under her jeans-clad bottom and one around her waist.

She finally drew her mouth away and gasped for air.

He took advantage of the moment to drag in a breath.

"How dare you," she repeated in a whisper, letting her forehead fall to his shoulder, "make Darrell look like such jerk?"

"I didn't—"

She tipped her head back again to look into his eyes. "How dare you have no training with children and still know how to deal with them better than he does?"

"All I—"

"How dare you—" her eyelashes fell languidly,

then lifted "—make my heartbeat accelerate by just walking into a kitchen with a pile of dirty dishes?"

He pressed her even closer and wrested control on the moment, kissing her soundly. He had the answer.

"Because I love you," he said.

Chapter Ten

The children played all afternoon, no races or competitions planned to impinge on their freedom.

The men played football. Darrell reminded everyone of the formal rules of play, but he was ignored. They all finally came into the kitchen desperate for coffee and looking like the less-than-perfectly conditioned but still fascinatingly male second string of some lesser-known team.

Darrell stayed to make a fresh pot of coffee. When Ruth Naomi and Beebee appeared, Darrell clearly targeted for the promised piece of Ruth Naomi's mind, Susan escaped.

Leftovers were hauled out late in the afternoon and everyone reconvened in the building. Someone had brought a guitar, and dads and kids sprawled out in the soft furniture around the room to sing.

They started with children's songs, camp songs, Disney show tunes. The children sang heartily.

As the children wore down and night fell, the guitarist turned to love songs. Ross and Flynn placed camp lights on several of the picnic tables as the crowd quieted and children drifted off to sleep.

Susan sat on a lumpy brown sofa beside Aaron, the two younger boys in their laps, the two older ones flanking them. Paul's eyes closed sleepily. John was awake but nearly comatose with contentment.

Susan listened to the guitarist sing in a raspy tenor about love that could not be denied and felt as though the song had been written for her. It was one thing to feel that she was loved, but it was something else entirely to hear the words spoken while enfolded in an embrace that could melt bones with its sincerity.

She knew now that she couldn't simply let Aaron leave and still believe that life could go on with any normalcy. And if the compromise couldn't be Aaron's because so many more people were affected by his decisions, then it would have to be hers.

She leaned into Aaron's shoulder as he tightened his arm around her, the children all entangled with them, and knew this was the way it should be. They were becoming the family she'd always wanted for herself as a child, and the one she wanted for the boys.

She looked around the room at the single fathers, eyes closed or staring moodily as they listened to the lyrics, and hoped Elaine and Darcie would be able to find solutions for all of them.

Ruth Naomi and Beebee, seated across from each other at the far end of a picnic table, caught her eye and toasted her with their coffee mugs.

She didn't have to wonder what their gesture was saying to her. She heard it loud and clear. In fact, it echoed in her mind the rest of the night and the whole way home.

The children showered and went to bed without complaint, exhausted after their busy day.

Susan and Beebee packed lunches for the following day, then Susan shooed Beebee off to bed while Aaron took Burgie out before locking up for the night.

Susan piled her hair atop her head and climbed into the tub for a shower, tired from the long, illuminating day.

She laughed to herself at how handsome and interesting Darrell had looked, and at how completely insufferable she'd found him. It was clear that organizational skills, though admirable under some circumstances, weren't everything. And sometimes not what the moment required at all.

Aaron's generosity and indulgence, which had so worried her when he'd first arrived, she now saw as a ray of affection under which the boys had blossomed. Unlike Darrell's children, who might blossom despite him, but who might never know what it was like to enjoy a moment that wasn't intended to teach them something, that could simply be enjoyed because it *was*.

And Aaron loved *her,* the tool freak who'd rather build than shop.

She was thinking she should speak to him about what she intended before they went to bed. There'd barely been time to exchange a word since they'd gotten home.

But she wanted to tell him that the president of the cable network was planning to attend the Hearth and Home Show in New York, and that she'd try to find the right moment to ask him if he'd consider a change in the format of her show. Maybe a new location in Seattle so that she could still fulfill her contract.

She turned off the shower, then pulled aside the curtain to reach for her terry-cloth robe—and...

She found herself eye to eye with Aaron. He stood near the tub, holding her robe open for her to step into. And he didn't look as though he had conversation in mind.

His eyes ran over her body still beaded with water, a soft smile curving his lips as he finally raised his gaze to her face.

"How dare you," he said quietly "be even more magnificent than I'd imagined?"

"I—"

"Shh," he whispered, helping her into the robe, then picking her up into his arms. "That doesn't require an answer. I just checked and all the boys are sound asleep and Beebee's light is out. Let's not risk waking anybody."

"Okay. But I wanted to—"

"Shh." He kissed her into silence, then carried her out of the bathroom, down the hall, the stairs, and into the family room and his sofa bed.

He stood her on her feet and rubbed her arms through the robe to dry them. He did her back, her hips—which made her forget for a moment who and where she was—then her legs. When he used the hem of the fabric to rub up along the inside of her knee, she felt everything inside her warm and melt, collecting in a thick pool deep inside her. She no longer had conversation in mind, either.

Then he pulled at the half knot she'd made of the

belt and said quietly, his mouth against hers, "You didn't say that *you* love *me*."

"Didn't I?" she whispered, awareness beginning to spin.

He slipped his hand inside her robe. "No, you didn't." One went to her back, the other to her hip, and he pulled her closer with it.

She shrugged off the robe, then looped her arms around his neck. "I guess I just felt it so deeply—" she kissed him slowly, dipping her tongue inside, nipping at his lip "—I thought I'd said it. I love you, Aaron. I love you."

HE DIDN'T HAVE TO KNOW anything more. Since that moment in the kitchen when she'd fulfilled his wildest fantasies and dragged him to a dark corner and kissed him, he'd known he wasn't going to be able to go back to Seattle without leaving his heart and soul here.

And contrary to popular belief, a shell of a man could not run a successful business. At least not his. Every moment of every day problems arose that involved people, and it was impossible to deal with people without feeling. And feeling required heart.

Right now that heart thumped and thudded and caused all his body's processes to race.

And while his body worked overtime, his brain seemed to be slowing down. Thought was choked out by sensation as Susan's finger slipped up under his sweatshirt and moved over his back, pausing to study the jut of his shoulder blades, the muscle at his sides.

He yanked off the sweatshirt as her hand moved

around the front of him. She caressed his pectoral muscles, then his abdominals.

"When do you have time to work out?" she asked in flattering wonder, letting her fingertips run over his ridged stomach.

He had to think. "Ah...gym. Near the office."

But he didn't want to talk about himself. He cupped her breast in his hands and her eyelashes fluttered, her hands stilled on his chest and she leaned into him with a little sigh of pleasure.

The tips of her breasts beaded in his palms, and her pleasure in his touch intensified his longing for her.

She unbuckled his belt, but hesitated over the zipper. She seemed suddenly shy or uncertain.

Panic threatened him. She wasn't changing her mind, was she?

"Aren't you frightened?" she asked, her finger, which rested on the waistband of his jeans, sending very erotic sensations against his stomach.

He was a little confused by the question. "Of you?" he asked.

She smiled. "Of love. If you can believe other people's experiences, it'll rob you of the focus you used to have. It'll dissipate your energy, diminish—"

He put a hand over her mouth, amused by the very idea. "I don't think so," he said. "I don't think it dissipates or diminishes anything. In fact I feel right now as though I could *lend* energy to a nuclear-power plant. Why? Are you afraid of it?"

"Not afraid exactly," she admitted with a candor he was beginning to admire and appreciate. "It's just a little harder to be reckless when four little lives are now attached to mine and affected by everything I do.''

He wasn't sure he liked her choice of words. ''Reckless? That implies that I present some kind of danger to you. You have to know I'd never hurt you or the boys.''

She nodded. ''You wouldn't want to. But making love is going to deepen what's already too significant for safety.''

''Then…you'd rather not?'' He held his breath.

She smiled in self-deprecation. ''If I had any sense, I'd think twice. But I don't.''

He dropped his hands from her and folded them over his chest, calling himself all kinds of a fool. But he didn't like where this was going. ''Then maybe you'd better think twice,'' he said, ''because I don't want this to be just a foolish reaction to something you can't control. I want you in my bed because making love with me is what you want to do tonight more that anything in this world.''

She put a hand on his arm, her eyes troubled. ''It is, Aaron. I was trying to tell you that behaving responsibly is what I do. And this feels so good that my brain thinks it's *ir*responsible. Silly huh?''

''What does your heart think?''

She reached up to plant a light kiss on his lips, hers smiling. ''It's calling you. Can you hear it?''

''Of course I can. And my heart's been yours since I met you.'' he kissed her lightly, tenderly. ''You can have my body, too, if you want it.''

''Oh, I want it.''

In a moment she'd helped relieve him of jeans and

briefs and simply stared at him, a pink blush rising up from her breast to color her neck and her cheeks.

"How dare you?" she asked, her voice frail, "be even more magnificent than my—"

He kissed her before she could finish, tired of talking. He wrapped his arms around her and, planting a knee on the bed, eased her into the middle of the pillows.

She brought him down with her, her arms around his neck.

They touched, kissed, explored and explored again. He rained kisses from her chin to her toes and she kept pace with him, giving everything he gave, exploring where he touched.

When she tried to outpace him, he pinned her to the mattress with a hand at her waist.

"Don't do that," he cautioned "if you want this to last into the sunrise."

She giggled, giddy with happiness. "Now that's a bit of a boast, isn't it?"

"We'll talk about it over breakfast."

"Honestly, Aaron. If...*ah!*"

His touch inside her dissolved her blurred sensations of a moment ago, and the whole world seemed to twist into sharp focus. The mysteries of life were distilled into one simple truth. *Love is everything. Love makes you feel like this.*

She tried to describe it to herself to help alleviate the torturous tension. Pleasure? Anguish? Expectation? Anticipation?

Her hands fussed at him, trying to hurry the relief he seemed determined to keep at bay.

He took both her hands in one of his and held them above her head.

"Easy," he said softly, planting a kiss between her breasts as he continued his delicious torture. "This isn't about being in charge, or being responsible, or even being good. It's just about letting it happen."

She eyed him threateningly as he made her mindless with need, letting her reach the fine edge of fulfillment, then drawing her back again until she thought she would die of the tension.

"I'll get you!" she warned on a gasp.

"I'll hold you to that," he promised, then tucking her close, let her have her way.

Pleasure came at her in a rush, like a storm surge or a hurricane wind. Though she already lay in his arms, she felt as though it toppled her, tumbled her, then rolled her over for good measure, so disorienting was the power of it.

Before she'd quite recovered, Aaron tried to rise over her, but she was still filled with the power of the experience, and pushed back.

"Suzie I want—" he began, but she put a hand over his mouth as she climbed astride his waist.

She remove her hand just long enough to kiss him for the "Suzie." No one had ever called her Suzie. Then she silenced him again as she raked her fingernails gently over his ribs.

"This isn't about what *you* want, Bradley," she said, drunk with power, delirious with the love he'd made, wanting to give it back with that same exquisite perfection. "I said I'd get you, remember? So just relax while I teach *you* to just let it happen."

And she gave it a good try. She taunted him with

her fingernails from his shoulders to his knees, then revisited all the places where she'd gotten a particularly interesting reaction.

"Suze," he said, his voice a little breathless. "Just let me…"

A well-placed kiss turned the words to a groan and made him powerless to protest as she planted kisses everywhere.

"I don't…" he began again.

This time she blew a little breath of air across his shoulders.

He swore.

She drew featherlight kisses down the middle of his body over his navel, across his hipbones, but was stopped just short of her objective.

He caught her thighs in his hands, held her in place and entered her with a skillful tilt of his hips.

She retained control for just a few seconds, then lost it when the tempest of a moment ago threatened again and she let him roll them over.

They came together in a vigorous shattering of body boundaries. She could no longer identify her flesh, her heartbeat, her breath. It mingled with his, was lost in his, so that their pleasure was a single thing they shared equally and owned together. With its force so focused, it went on and on and on.

AARON DECIDED that he'd lied to Susan when he'd answered her question just before he'd made love to her. He *was* afraid of love.

Judging by the way this felt, he'd just never been in love before. So maybe he hadn't lied; he'd simply been wrong because he hadn't really known what he was talking about.

That is, he'd *known* he'd loved her, but he'd never *made* love to a woman he'd loved before. He hadn't understood how different it would make him feel, how the power translated itself in tenderness, and how the quest for pleasure became the need to give pleasure.

The world as he knew it stood on its ear.

It was weird how comfortable that was. As long as he didn't wonder how they were going to solve the bicoastal situation. Susan must have resolved something in her mind if she'd been willing to make love with him.

"I was thinking…" she said, as though reading his mind. Her upper body was sprawled over his, one of her legs entangled with one of his. "The president of my cable network is going to New York for the show. They do a lot of schmoozing and partying. I'll try to find the right moment to ask him if I can move the show to Seattle."

Aaron was stunned. It was what he'd wanted, but he'd never expected her to try to compromise with such grace.

"You'd do that?" he asked in disbelief.

She studied his expression, then frowned worriedly. "Don't you want me to?"

He laughed and hugged her close, turning so that he could tuck her comfortably against him. "Of course I do. I just didn't think *you* wanted to. You think they'll go for it?"

"I have no idea. I don't know whether to be hopeful about it or not."

"When is that trip?"

She hooked her arm around his waist and held tightly. "This coming Friday. I'll be gone three whole days—it'll feel like an eternity. Will you and Beebee manage okay, or should I have Ruth Naomi look in on you?"

"We'll be fine. If I have any trouble, I'll just hit another Daddy Club meeting."

"I was afraid the two divas weren't going to like each other at first," she said with a smile in her voice, "then Darrell messed with their potluck dishes and I think it brought them together."

"I expected you to like him," Aaron said, able to admit that now. "What happened?"

"Oh, he was just a pill. He's more compulsive than organized. I thought I'd like that attention to detail but it made me crazy. You with your unbounded ability to seize the moment—" She raised her head to smile into his eyes with deviltry. "—and fill it with something expensive seems much more sane to me."

She heaved a gusty sigh. "I wonder how the kids will feel about moving?"

"Hard to tell."

"I don't think we should say anything until I get a reaction from my boss."

"Right. What about the addition you planned with Flynn?"

"I was thinking about that. Shouldn't we go through with it? It'll delay our putting the house on the market, but it'll make it more valuable."

He kissed the top of her head. "Very sensible."

"There." She sighed again and snuggled closer.

"This relationship's going very well so far, don't you think?"

"Yes, I do."

But scared to death and ecstatically happy, he thought, were difficult emotional states to sustain side by side.

SUSAN HUGGED JOHN, then Paul who both wore long faces. "I'll be gone only three days," she said for the fourth time since breakfast, "and I'll bring you all a present when I come back."

Paul smiled fractionally. John remained glum.

Susan hugged Ringo in Beebee's arms, then turned around to hug George—who wasn't there.

"Where's George?" she asked John.

"Under his bed."

"What?"

"Dad's trying to get him out. He doesn't want you to go."

John had been calling Aaron "Dad" since the day he'd made the decision the first day of school. Susan had stopped trying to correct him.

With a quick glance at the clock Susan ran up the stairs to George's and Ringo's room. Aaron lay on his stomach on the blue carpet, his tight backside neatly outlined in his old jeans.

"But she's not taking a plane." He seemed to be speaking to the underside of the bed. "She's going by train."

"Trains have assidents, too!" the voice under the bed wailed.

"That's true," Aaron replied reasonably, "but a lot of people get where they're going safely."

"My other mom didn't!"

"I know. But this is different."

"How come?"

"Because she only has to go a short distance, and the weather's very good for traveling today."

"I want her to stay here."

"But she has to go, George. She promised people she would be there, and she never breaks a promise."

"She promised me she'd always be here!"

Aaron rose to his knees to smile ruefully at Susan. "Good going," he said wryly. "I almost had him."

Susan lay down on her stomach and found the little tearstained face under the bed. Her heart twisted.

"George," she said calmly, "when I said I would always be here, I meant that my love for you would always be here, but sometimes I would have to leave someone else in my place to take care of you. Beebee will be here."

"I want *you!*"

"And Daddy will be here."

She didn't realize what she'd said until the words were out of her mouth. It had become such a natural thing—Mommy and Daddy and their four little boys.

She had to go to New York and make that work.

George crawled out from under the bed. "You promise you're going to come right back?" he demanded as she rose to her knees and took him in her arms.

"I promise. And I'll bring you a big present."

He frowned, as though offended that she thought he could be bought. "I just want you to come home."

She hugged him tightly. "I'll come home. I promise."

George looked up at Aaron. "And you're gonna stay, right?"

"Right. I'm gonna stay."

"Okay." George went back under the bed.

Susan looked up at Aaron, mystified.

George emerged a moment later with her makeup case. "I thought you wouldn't go if you didn't have this. It gots your hair spray in it."

They made the train station with barely five minutes to spare.

"I'm going to miss you," Susan said, holding desperately to Aaron. Three days stretched ahead of her like an eternity. What if she couldn't take the show to Seattle? What would she do?

"This is to make sure you think about me once in a while. At least every time you wave down a taxi." Aaron pulled something out of the pocket of his raincoat and slipped it onto her finger.

A marquis-cut diamond on a wide gold band worked with open hearts caught the overhead light and almost blinded her.

"Aaron!"

The conductor called, "All aboard!"

"Will you marry me?" Aaron asked, running her to the train.

"But—"

"I seize the moment, remember?" he said, quoting her. "And fill it with expensive things."

The conductor called again. A redcap took her bag.

"I love you," she said, rising on tiptoe to kiss him. "And I'd love to marry you."

"Good." He walked her to the open door and helped her up the steps.

She turned to lean down to him, desperate for one more touch. The train began to pull away.

"Make your boss see things our way!" he called over the sound, walking to keep up.

"I will! I love you!"

"I love you, too! Call us!"

The train picked up speed. He blew her a kiss and she blew it back, feeling like the brokenhearted heroine in some war movie.

Three days, she told herself bracingly as she found a seat, was hardly a lengthy death-defying separation.

Although it felt like that. She remembered the older boys' long faces, George's pleas that she return, the love in Aaron's eyes as he put the ring on her finger.

She put a hand to her fluttering heart at the sudden realization of how truly vulnerable she'd become.

Chapter Eleven

Aaron was mopping the kitchen floor when he heard the doorbell. Great. The older boys were in school, and Beebee had taken George and Ringo grocery shopping.

He leaned the mop against the counter, stepped carefully over the wet floor and went to answer it.

It was Micah.

"I asked Paulette out," he said without preamble as Aaron poured coffee and pointed him to the kitchen table, cautioning him to watch his step.

"Great. Cookies?"

"Sure." Micah pulled off an all-weather jacket, hung it over the back of his chair and sat. "Where's Susan?"

Aaron told him about the trip to New York as he put a plate of Beebee's peanut-butter cookies in the middle of the table. "She'll be back Monday afternoon. What's the matter? You look…worried."

"I am." Micah stared into his cup, his frown deepening as he looked up at Aaron and sighed. "Women make me nervous. I mean…when you consider them seriously. They worry about a lot of things I never gave a rip about before. Don't they?''

Aaron crossed his arms on the table and leaned toward him. ''Yeah, I guess. But what are you talking about?''

Micah drew another breath and studied his spoon as though it had the potential to hurt him. Then he put it in his cup and stirred, though he'd added no cream or sugar to his coffee.

''I thought you'd understand,'' he said. ''You stayed because of a woman you'd known only a couple of days.''

Aaron nodded encouragingly.

''Well, I spent just a couple of hours with Paulette, and though I've never ever considered marriage and children and all that cutesy stuff that goes with it...''

''Yeah?''

''I'm thinking about it now. I'm not going to rush her. I'll give this all the time it needs. But I'm really worried about— Am I nuts? Have pod people taken over my brain? And if I'm not and they haven't, what would she see in a broken-down road rat?''

Aaron rolled his eyes. ''First of all, you *are* nuts. I'm surprised you even have to ask.'' At Micah's raised eyebrow, he went on with grin. ''You're not broken down. Come on. You always look like the cover of *Cigar Aficionado* or something. And she seemed as taken with you as you did with her.''

Micah looked pathetically hopeful. ''She did?''

''She did.''

''So you think it'd work?''

''Why not?''

Micah seemed to consider it, then shook his head,

clearly afraid to put too much faith in Aaron's optimism. Then he asked, "What are you doing about Starscape?"

"Nothing. Susan's coming with me—provided she can move the show."

"Wow."

"That's what I said. But getting back to you…"

Again Micah stirred nothing into his coffee. "You and I are kind of in the same boat, you know. I mean we've had careers that are our lives, not just ways to make a living. How do you put that aside for a family? I'm worried about that. I mean, should I sell the Knight Club? And if I do, will it make me cranky and hard to live with?"

Aaron pushed the cookies toward him. "Here," he said. "You need a little sugar. I'd wait to see how she reacts to all this before you plan to sell anything. She might find life in a nightclub as exciting as you do. She might love the regulars, the camaraderie, the high spirits."

"But can you be in that kind of business when you have children?"

"I don't see why not. Morticians have children. Dogcatchers have children."

Aaron laughed at Micah's horror at being so compared. "Well, for God's sake, Micah! You run a great place."

"Maybe I should consider a restaurant or a small inn. Fine dining, you know?"

"Just wait and see what happens."

Micah took a cookie and snapped it in two. He consumed one half in a single swallow. "Things are looking pretty good for you, then. You don't have to give up anything?''

"Depends on what happens in New York."

"If she can't move the show, what then?"

"I don't know. We'll see."

Micah smiled. "You can always come and wait tables for me at my inn."

Aaron laughed. "Thanks. I might have to take you up on that."

Aaron had just walked Micah to the door and waved him off when the telephone rang. It was the elementary-school principal. She sounded harried.

A niggle of dread ran along his spine.

"Mr. Bradley, these things seem so…so…" She sighed. He could imagine her wringing her hands. "But if we don't take them seriously, we have to answer to the school board and all the other parents, who—"

"Mrs. Harris," he interrupted, his panic increasing with her disconnected explanation. "Please tell me what happened."

"Well…" he heard the beginnings of sound, but it ended in an exasperated groan. "Mr. Bradley," she started again, her voice a little firmer this time, "I've had to suspend Paul from school."

He was grateful Susan was out of town.

"Why?" he asked with forced calm.

"He kissed Whitney Garwood in the resource center."

For a full ten seconds Aaron was speechless. It was on the tip of his tongue to berate such a decision for what surely had to be a completely innocent gesture on the part of a six-year old.

Then he remembered that six-year-olds grew up to be sixteen-year-olds and that important lessons had to be learned early on.

"Forcibly?" he asked.

"I wouldn't say forcibly," Mrs. Harris replied. "He just took her by surprise. I can't allow that, Mr. Bradley. The school board would hang me out to dry."

"I understand, Mrs. Harris. I'll be right there."

The principal was lecturing the boy on the respect today's woman required from today's man when Aaron arrived.

"He's suspended for three days," Mrs. Harris said, handing Aaron a stack of books and paperwork. "I'd appreciate it if you could explain the problem to him during that time. And this is his schoolwork for Monday and Tuesday."

Paul looked worried and confused as he sat in a straight-back chair next to Mrs. Harris's desk, his legs dangling.

She smiled sympathetically at Paul as he slid to his feet. "You think about all the things we discussed, Paul," she said, walking them to the door of her office. "And we'll see you Wednesday, all right?"

"All right." He took Aaron's hand and allowed himself to be led out to the van.

Aaron waited until they were home before he broached the subject of Paul's suspension. They sat across from each other at the kitchen table.

"Do you understand what happened?" Aaron asked handing Paul a cup of cocoa.

Paul sighed and gave him a grim look. "I guess in

school you're not supposed to get to know girls the way you got to know Susan.''

Aaron was unable to interpret Paul's meaning. ''I don't understand.''

Paul took a sip of the chocolate. He swallowed and drew a deep breath. ''Susan said that when you were kissing her, you were trying to get to know her. That's what I was doing with Whitney.''

Oh boy. ''I see. Well, you know, there are a lot of things that are okay for adults to do that aren't okay for kids.''

''Like smoking and drinking.''

''Right.''

''But a kiss is nice. Like a present.'' Paul smiled, sincere in his interpretation. Aaron detected a lethal charm in the making. ''I don't see why that's bad. Whitney even said she liked it.''

Aaron groped for the right words. ''A kiss is like a present,'' he said, handing Paul a napkin, ''and that's why you have to pick the right time and the right place, and never do it in school where you're supposed to be concentrating on learning.''

''But I was. I was looking at this book about flowers, and Jake Farewell said I was a sissy 'cause...I liked them. But Whitney said that wasn't true 'cause her dad has a flower shop and he's not a sissy.'' He smiled again. ''I think that means she likes me.''

''I'm sure she does. You're a nice guy. Everybody likes you. But maybe she was just doing a nice thing by defending you because Jake was picking on you.''

''She gave me her Sweetarts, Dad.'' Paul seemed to consider that conclusive evidence.

Aaron tried not to react to being called Dad. Not

because he didn't like it, but because he did. He never corrected John when he did it, but preferred to make as little out of it as possible. The ultimate end of this relationship was still on dangerous ground.

"Not everyone's willing to give away his or her candy," he said. "So if she really does like you, that's all the more reason to make sure you treat her as if she's very special. A kiss is something a man shares with a woman, not something he just takes."

Paul frowned over that. "I was trying to tell her I like her, too."

Aaron nodded. "Next time try to find the right words to say that and save kissing for when you're older."

Paul grimaced. "Do I have to wait until I'm as old as you?"

Aaron would have disputed that remark, except that he *was* feeling ancient at the moment.

"No, you don't have to be quite this old. But old enough to know how to ask politely and to accept it gracefully if she says no, or to make her feel really special if she says yes."

Paul leaned back against his seat, running his fingers along the edge of the table. "Do you think Susan will be mad at me? You know, 'cause she's a girl and everything?"

"We'll just explain that you were confused about the etiquette."

"Etiquette?"

"The good manners."

"Oh. Are you mad at me?"

"No. But now that you understand, I'll expect you not to do it again."

Paul nodded seriously. "No kissing." He grinned at Aaron. "Too bad. It was really nice."

Aaron kept a straight face with difficulty. "I know. It's even nicer when you're older, so just be patient and wait for the right time, okay?"

"Okay."

IN HER SIGNATURE COVERALLS from *Susan's Workshop* Susan demonstrated Legacy Tools in the cavernous exhibition hall all afternoon Friday. At night she went home to her lonely hotel room and called home.

"The Bradley residence," John answered.

Susan was surprised by his formality—and by the name he'd chosen. Of course, the boys' name was Bradley, too.

"Hi, John, it's Susan. What lovely telephone manners you have."

"We learned that in school yesterday," he said. "But Paul had bad manners and he got suspended!"

"What?" she demanded, pulling her shoes off her aching feet. "What do you mean, suspended?"

"John, I told you I'd explain that when she got home," she heard Aaron's admonishing voice over John's. "Why don't you get into your pajamas?"

Then he was on the line. "Susan?"

"What happened?"

"Paul kissed a little girl in the library because she'd done something nice for him and he was trying to show his appreciation," he explained. "The rule is he has to be suspended for three days."

"But—!"

"I know. But the school has to take it seriously.

We talked about it when I picked him up and I think he understands.''

"I can't believe it!''

"He was trying to get to know her better,'' he said, his voice rich with amusement. "He says you told him that's what we were doing when he found us kissing.''

She groaned. "You mean it's *my* fault?''

He laughed. "Of course not. I think it's the fault of a nimble little mind that's a couple of years ahead of his physical development. And I can't buy us out of this one with an Island Treasure disk. But don't worry. Everything's okay.''

"But our child is suspended in the first grade!'' Lost in the ignominy of Paul's punishment, Susan didn't realize what she'd said until the word echoed around her. *Our child.*

There was silence for an instant on the other end, then Aaron said bracingly, "He'll survive. And I don't think the little girl was too traumatized. She claims to have liked it, according to Paul. So we'll just live with it, and he promises not to do it again. How are *you* doing?''

"I'm fine. Just tired. How are the other boys?''

"Everybody's good. Ringo even walked around the yard with me today when I took Burgie out. I think that's the first time I haven't had to carry him since I've been here.''

"Great.'' The children were thriving. She had to make sure that continued. But the network brass had wandered back and forth in a large group all day long, stopping occasionally to watch her demonstration and to listen while she answered questions. "I haven't had a chance to get Mr. Jekel alone yet. But I will."

"Good." His deep voice was a balm to her weary spirit. "I miss you," he said, his voice dipping an octave and taking on an intimacy that was like a touch.

"I miss you, too," she whispered. "I'll meet you on the couch when I get home."

"It's a date."

She was shocked and delighted an hour later to answer a knock on her door and find Paulette standing there. She threw her arms around her and pulled her into the room.

"What are you doing here? I'm so glad to see you! God, New York is lonely!"

Paulette fell into a chair and kicked her shoes off. "And big! I'll bet people who live here don't need treadmills. I keep thinking I should come here more often so I don't act like such a hillbilly, but I still feel like Grandma Clampet on her rocking chair on top of all the luggage in the back of the car."

"I can offer you wine or club soda from the honor bar."

"Actually I'm here to take you out to dinner."

"Why?"

"In exchange for your lovelorn advice."

Susan snapped her finger in Paulette' face. "Hello-o. I'm a carpenter."

"You said it yourself on the show you did from Ruth Naomi's. Relationships are built, too, aren't they?"

SUSAN STARED AT PAULETTE in astonishment as the waiter placed large salads filled with exotic greens in front of them. He ground pepper on them, then walked away.

"Micah proposed?" Susan asked in disbelief.

Paulette nodded, carefully tossing her salad.

"After three dates?"

"Yes."

"But you've only known him two and half weeks. I mean, I like him. I think he's great. But..."

Paulette reached across the table to point the prongs of her fork at the ring on Susan's finger. "What's that?" The question was loaded with significance.

Susan tossed her hair. "It's an engagement ring," she said briskly. "And yes, Aaron and I haven't known each other much longer than you and Micah, but we've literally spent every waking moment in each other's company, and we share the care of four children. That solidifies a relationship pretty quickly."

Paulette sagged visibly, leaned back in her chair and fluttered her napkin. "I *am* crazy, aren't I?" she said. "I keep trying to tell myself that every relationship has its own pace and timing, and when it's right, it's right, no matter how long you've known each other. If someone is kind to you, makes you laugh and seems to enjoy you as much as you enjoy him, is there *ever* more than that no matter how long you wait?"

"That's pretty much it," Susan had to agree. "Except for children."

Paulette nodded. "He wants at least three." Her eyes lost focus suddenly and she smiled with silly indulgence. "But he's afraid a nightclub owner wouldn't make a good father. That a child wouldn't be proud to take him to show-and-tell. Isn't that cute?"

Susan found herself smiling, too. "So, you're considering his proposal?"

Paulette shook her head.

At Susan's confused expression, she giggled. "I've already accepted. I just had to see if you're as miserable away from Aaron as you are happy when he's around. That seems like a sign of a successful relationship to me." She picked up her fork again. "Interesting, isn't it, how we used to mourn the lack of good men and suddenly we've each got one? Sort of."

"Yes it is," Susan replied absorbing the news. "Are you going home tonight?"

Paulette shook her head. "I'm staying for the meeting."

"What meeting?"

"The one about your show." Paulette looked up from examining the roll basket. "Mr. Jekel was supposed to tell you about it today."

Susan shook her head in concern. "No one's told me anything. They just hung around the Legacy Tools booth a lot of the time and watched me work my tail off. What do they want?"

"I don't know. I was just told to be here."

"Do you think ratings are down?"

"No. I know for a fact they're up."

Susan smiled at the possibilities. "Maybe we're going to get raises." Then she frowned. "Or they want to replace me with that Heidi from *Home Im-*

provement because of the Hardware and Muffins show.'' The audience might have liked the intrusion of children, but the network brass usually frowned on the unexpected.

''I don't think so. We'll just have to wait and see.''

Susan didn't understand how Paulette could even entertain that strategy. Of course, Paulette hadn't intended to arrange an impromptu meeting herself to propose a change in the program at the same time that Mr. Jekel had called a meeting with plans of his own.

Susan could not dismiss an unsettling sense of trouble. Big trouble.

JOSHUA JEKEL LOOKED more like a Mafia don than a businessman. He was not very tall, thick around the middle, had a beakey nose and a predilection for dark shirts and ties and smelly cigars.

He stopped by the Legacy Tools booth Saturday afternoon and invited Susan to dinner with his team, with the tool company's people and Paulette.

''We'll meet here when the show closes tonight,'' he said. ''Legacy's limo will pick us up.''

She felt excitement mingled with trepidation. Whatever was going on here, she guessed, it was going to blow holes in her plan to sell Jekel on moving the show to Seattle.

Knowing there'd be no time to call home between closing the show and leaving for dinner, she called in the middle of the afternoon and got the answering machine.

She left her love and reminded John of the book report he had due on Monday. Then she went back to work, feeling nervous and lonely and dreading the dinner.

But by the time she entered the nook of the bistro's dining room, she'd smiled at the collection of network and tool-company executives gathered around the table. They used to intimidate her until she'd taken on the care of four boys. Now she considered herself invincible.

She and Paulette sat side by side in the group of men of varying ages and were fussed over and cosseted for most of the evening.

Susan was just beginning to think she could live with this kind of treatment when Jekel pulled several sheets of paper out of his breast pocket and began quoting statistics regarding *Susan's Workshop*'s ratings and the sponsor's report of increased sales.

Unless she misunderstood, she thought, he was claiming her to be the cable network's answer to Oprah Winfrey.

She couldn't quite believe her ears. Until she'd taken the boys she'd felt as if she was still learning to put the show together, even though it was in its second year.

She'd researched more complicated but interesting projects with the complete conviction that women wanted to make more than flower boxes and mailboxes. She'd worked on simplifying and smoothing out her presentation, on adapting professional techniques to home projects, knowing that though women's hands weren't quite as strong as a man's, they were better suited to fine work and easily capable of the finishing work fine carpentry required.

Since she'd taken the boys, she hadn't had time to

think at all. She'd operated on instinct and what her mail told her her audience enjoyed.

Jekel tucked his paper back into his breast pocket and smiled benevolently at Susan. "We have big plans for you, young lady. And so does Legacy Tools."

Susan felt her insides begin to tremble, that twin-headed excitement/trepidation thing again.

"We'd like to give you five days a week, if you think you can handle it," he said, "and your audience loves what you did at that Toast and Tools place."

"Hardware and Muffins, sir," one of his assistants corrected.

"Right. If the owner of that place is in agreement, we'd like you to do an entire season on projects for small businesses. You can renovate that place show by show."

Ruth Naomi would be ecstatic.

"We're also planning to spin off the Daddy Club that got involved in that show. The audience's reaction was off the charts. We'd like that Neil Graber to host for us—he certainly has the credentials. And if Mrs. Steadwell is willing to let us film from..." He turned to his assistant for the name.

"Hardware and Muffins."

"...Hardware and Muffins, we'll slot them right after you, and you can just walk across the show and intro Graber. What do you think?"

Susan really tried to think, but found it impossible. Every neuron in her brain had closed off in shock.

"You haven't told her about the ad campaign for Legacy," Milton Fuller, the CEO of Legacy, said.

Jekel deferred to Fuller. "Why don't you do that?"

Fuller nodded and leaned toward her conspiratorially, as though they were alone at the table of twelve.

"We want to use you in an ad campaign, Susan," he said. "On all our stations and in print. We'll talk money afterward, but I think you'll be pleased with what we're offering."

"Speaking of money," Jekel said, "did I mention that we're quadrupling your salary?"

When her mouth fell open, everyone laughed. "And Paulette's too, of course. We researched other talents with your size audience, and we went a little over their salaries to prove that we have plans for you for the long term. We'll just lob next year off the current contract and start fresh with a new three-year deal."

"If you're in agreement with all this," Fuller said, "and can let us know by say tomorrow night, I have a photographer standing by to shoot you for our print campaign—that is, if you can clear your calendar to stay in New York until next Friday's show?"

"I...I..."

Paulette stopped Susan's stammering with an arm around her shoulders. "I think she's a little overwhelmed," she said. "We'll talk it over and she'll be in touch after the show closes tomorrow afternoon."

Everyone agreed, offered their congratulations, praised her success and left Paulette to walk her to the elevator.

Susan leaned against the handrail as the car went up, still completely stunned. "We had *what* kind of ratings?"

Paulette repeated the figure.

"And Legacy's sales have improved how much since advertising on our show?"

"Fifty-seven percent."

"Maybe people just didn't known they were there before."

"No, women just didn't know they could use them until you showed them what they could do with them and how."

"But—" Susan was beginning to feel faint "—the boys. I can't do five shows a week and give them what they need. I can't stay here until Friday. I can't…"

The elevator door parted and Paulette pushed her off the elevator and took her by the shoulders. "You're stuck on a *can't* track, honey. Just be quiet and draw a few deep breaths. Why don't you have a glass of wine, give Aaron a call and see what he says?"

Aaron.

Susan looked down at her ring. It winked back at her. She was engaged to Aaron. He would hate this. He couldn't stay and she…she…

She let herself think the truth. This was what she'd always dreamed of. This was the kind of success she'd worked toward before the boys had come into her life. This was her just reward for all those years of harassment when she'd worked construction.

Her heart sank at the realization that she no longer was the same woman who'd blundered into a successful career in television. She was a mother now, and her job was to provide what Becky's and Dave's boys needed—what *her* boys needed.

And if she stayed, Aaron would have to go without her—because that was the way it was.

She'd just about made up her mind not to call Aaron, to brood about it all night and call Jekel in the morning and tell him she couldn't do it, when Paulette handed her the telephone receiver.

"He's on the line," she said.

Susan put the phone to her ear. "Aaron?" she asked.

"Hi, sweetheart," he said, then asked instantly. "What's the matter? Something wrong?"

"No," she said quickly, wishing desperately that he was here beside her, instead of sixty miles away. "Paulette and I just came out of a meeting with the bosses, and they think we're wonderful. So we felt like boasting to someone."

Paulette gave her a scolding look, then waggled her fingers at her in a "tell him, tell him!" gesture.

Susan turned away from her.

"Well, that's unanimous," Aaron said, "because everyone here thinks you're pretty wonderful, too."

"Thank you," she said, letting the sound of his voice soothe her like a balm. "How are the boys?"

"Great. They want to go to church tomorrow to pray for your safe return. Beebee's coming, too."

"Thank you for doing that, Aaron. It's good for them."

"Hey. We do what we must, right?" he teased.

That, she thought, was very true.

She spoke briefly to all the boys, said good-night to Aaron and went to bed with his "I love you" still echoing in her ear.

But she couldn't sleep. She stared at the ceiling for several hours, accepting what she had to do, but accepting, also, that she wasn't quite big enough to cheerfully ignore the missed opportunity.

She thought with new respect about a few of the fathers in the Daddy Club who'd refused promotions and even forsworn careers in the interest of their increased obligations.

She'd gotten up to make tea in her tiny kitchen when she heard a light rap on her door. She went to the peephole and saw a distorted version of Aaron's face.

She tore the door open and threw herself into his arms. She was horrified when she burst into tears.

AARON KICKED THE DOOR closed behind him and wrapped his arms around Susan, alarmed and somehow relieved by this apparent loss of her customary control. She always made him feel as though he had to be as strong and as competent as she was, and he wasn't sure he had it in him.

Paulette's phone call had scared the hell out of him. He still hadn't quite recovered.

"Paulette called me after you hung up," he said rubbing her back. "She told me about what went on at the meeting. Seems you're a hot property."

He led her to the sofa and they sat, his arm around her, holding her close. He gave her his handkerchief and she eventually stopped crying. Her tear-filled eyes scanned his face.

"I'm sorry Paulette did that," she said. "She had no right."

"You didn't tell me the truth," he scolded. "Someone had to."

"It isn't the truth until I agree to the plan. At least, it isn't *my* truth. And I'm not going to do it."

"Do you want to?"

"I can't."

"That's not what I asked."

She gave him a dark look for forcing the issue.

"Yes I want to. But they want to make me part of the plan for the next few years. They want to center an ad campaign on me and help spin off a Daddy Club show, for heaven's sake! Talk about a rock and a hard place!"

"Paulette told me," he said, but he wasn't sure she even heard him.

"I can't spend that much time away from the boys. And with the direction in which they want to take things, there's no way I can sell them on moving the location to Seattle."

He opened his mouth to speak, but she cut him off. "No. Maybe I can convince them to get another hostess and they can still do a season at Hardware and Muffins."

"How many women around here do what you do?"

"I have connections. I'll find one."

"Susan," he said firmly, "I want you to do this. I thought about it all the way over here. I have to go back to Seattle for the launch of our new product, but then I think I can make a deal with Ted to take over for a year so I can stay here with the boys while you see how this goes. We don't want Hardware and Muffins or The Daddy Club to miss out on an opportunity like this. We'll reevaluate at the end of that time."

She couldn't believe her ears. She was sure there must be a million things to ask him, but she couldn't think of a single one.

"I called Beebee on my cell phone when I got the idea on the bridge somewhere over the Hudson, and she said she'd be happy to stay here with you to help out with the boys while I'm in Seattle. She even said that for as long as the show is at the hardware store, she'll pick them up from school and meet you there. They can do their homework over cocoa and muffins while you're working, and you'll be handy to each other if they need you.''

''But your business…''

''It'll survive, I'm sure. I like to think I'm its life's blood, but that isn't true. I work with brilliant resourceful people and they'll be fine without me. I'll just be a phone or a fax away, anyway.'' He smiled wryly. ''It hurts to say that, but I know it's the truth.''

''What if you end up… hating me?'' she asked anxiously. ''You've been great with the boys, but it's only been three weeks. You're talking about…''

He shrugged. ''And if you don't take this opportunity, you'll regret it for the rest of your life and end up hating *me*.'' He paused then said, ''You're going to do it. If you don't I'm not going to take you to bed with me and make love to you.''

She made a face at him. ''That's not the issue.''

''Well, let's make it the issue.''

''I'm not finished arguing.''

He kissed her soundly and lifted her into his arms. ''We'll finish in the morning.''

SUSAN HAD PLANNED to meet Paulette for an early breakfast, but was surprised when Micah sat in the booth beside Paulette, waiting for Susan and Aaron to arrive.

''Forgot to tell you,'' Aaron said as they slid into the opposite side. ''Micah was with me when Paulette called. He drove in with me.''

Susan glowered across the table at Paulette. ''I'd appreciate it,'' she said quietly, ''if you'd remember that you produce my show, not my life.''

"You were forgetting," Paulette argued, "that you're engaged. That means you should share life-altering decisions. I was just thinking of Aaron."

Susan smiled grudgingly, knowing Paulette had meant well. "Fine. Now you're such an expert on relationships that you think you can manage everyone's?"

Paulette held up her left hand and waggled her fingers. A large diamond on a simple gold band flashed brightly. Any remaining animosity was forgotten in hugs and handshakes.

Aaron and Micah wandered through the show, while Susan worked and Paulette became a part of the Jekel–Legacy Tool crew that came by from time to time, looking serious and talking quietly.

Jekel slipped in between visitors at one point to ask Susan if she could meet with them in the dinning room after the show closed.

She agreed.

"I understand your fiancé's here," he said. "Bring him with you. We have such a crowded couple of years planned here, that we want to make sure your home life fits in."

Then he was gone and a large man with a battery-powered Legacy drill he'd picked up off the display approached her, tripped over another visitor's feet and fell into her arms, the drill whirring above her left shoulder.

Half an inch closer, she thought, helping to steady him, and she could have worn a two-inch dowel in that ear. This was going to be a very long day.

Chapter Twelve

Susan accepted Jekel's offer. She told Milton Fuller she would like to be in his ad campaign but that she couldn't stay in New York until Friday.

"You know that I've just become guardian of my cousin's four boys, and I promised them I'd be gone only three days." She smiled winningly, determined to have this her way but afraid she might be undermining the whole unbelievable opportunity. "Perhaps we could reschedule for spring break when I can bring them with me?"

Fuller looked momentarily disappointed then nodded. "Of course. We want this to work for you. We all admire what you're doing. It probably even figures in your viewer appeal."

Susan smiled triumphantly at Aaron, then across the table at Paulette and Micah.

Jekel pointed his cigar at Paulette. "You're staying with us, aren't you, even after you're married?"

Paulette nodded firmly. "I am. Susan and I are a good team."

Jekel nodded. "The best we have. I can't tell you how happy we are with both of you." He put contracts on the table and handed each woman a pen. "If you'll just sign these, we'll all be on our way to fame and fortune."

Paulette reached for her contract, signed it and handed it back.

Susan pulled hers to her, opened it, then closed it again. She couldn't have explained what prevented her from signing her name.

"I'd like to take this home and look it over," she said, offering that winning smile again. "I'll mail it back."

Jekel looked suspicious. "Is something not the way you'd like it?"

"Everything's perfect," she insisted. "It's just that my head's spinning and I'd like to look this over when it's not. You have to understand what a surprise this has been to me."

"Certainly." Jekel slapped the table with the palm of his hand. "You do what feels comfortable. We want you to be happy."

AARON COULDN'T DECIDE just what was going on in Susan's mind. She should be thrilled, on top of the world, reeling with her success and the cable company's faith in her ability to attract even more.

Instead, she stared moodily out the window on the drive home. He wished Micah and Paulette hadn't stayed in New York. They would have broken the silence in the car. Susan just sat there, mute, the overalls and long braid she sported for the show replaced by a dark blue business suit and hair in a tidy knot.

Though, as a businessman himself, he applauded her professional appearance, he had difficulty relating to this persona. He was used to Susan in jeans, a sweater and ponytail, a woman who ran her home with an easy skill and a sense of humor that made it a happy place.

His mind flooded also with images of her as she'd been last night, her hair loose and flowing over him as she wore nothing at all but his ring.

But he couldn't think about that and drive, too.

"Anything you want to talk about?" he asked carefully, his eyes one the road.

"No," she replied. "You?"

"Yes." he sent her a quick glance that she intercepted with a small smile. "Why didn't you sign the contract?"

"Do you ever sign anything without reading it?" she challenged.

"No. But he said it was boiler-plate stuff, except for five shows, instead of one and a lot more money."

"Money isn't everything." Her tone was a little sanctimonious.

He sent her another glance, beginning to worry. "I know that. But money isn't really an issue either way, because we have enough."

"*You* have enough."

"I have… " he started to repeat her words, then stopped, too annoyed to finish. "I thought we were in this together. Have I done something to make you think I wouldn't share with you?"

"Of course not." She folded her arms and turned away from him, her body language saying, *just drop it.* "It isn't about money."

He never listened to body language. "Then, what is it about?"

"Aaron, would you please just drive!" she snapped.

He spotted a fast-food restaurant and pulled off the road and into the farthest corner of their parking lot. He unbuckled his seat belt and turned to her, panic and anger beginning to surface side by side. He drew a breath to control both.

"I'm your fiancé," he said, "not your chauffeur. What's the problem?"

She remained locked in her small corner of the front seat, her gaze resentful when it bounced off him. "There's no problem—at least, not yet. I guess I just can't believe there won't be."

"Well that's a pretty safe bet anytime, anywhere. But what *kind* of a problem?"

She finally unbuckled her belt and turned toward him, her eyes meeting and holding his with an odd reluctance he could not interpret as a good sign.

"My contract," she said, "is for three years. It was very generous of you to agree to give up a year to be with the boys, but it was just…one year. Then you said we'd reevaluate. What if you hate working from home? What if you find that being a full-time father gets on your nerves? You can love kids and still find they rob you of your sanity. What if I'm locked into a three-year contract and you've had it after a year?"

"I suggested a year," he said, fighting off temper in the interest of maintaining reason, "because I thought *you* might hate a five-day-a-week schedule. I don't remember putting conditions on my commitment to this. I said I'd do it."

She shook her head. "You're a great father, but I

can't see you being happy giving up your business so that I can—''

"That's because, you've confused me with *your* father! God, Susan! What do I have to do to convince you that I'm in this with you for the long haul? Apparently asking you to marry me wasn't enough.''

"Aaron, I love you. I do!'' She spread her arms in emphasis and her knuckles collided with the dash. She covered them with her other hand and held them to her, the blow seeming to diminish her head of steam. "I just think it'd be easier all around if I pack up the kids and we go with you.''

"No,'' he said surprising her into a wide-eyed stare. "No way. You're doing that because you don't trust me to do what I promised. You don't believe I'll live up to my half of the bargain.''

"You can't help it,'' she said in an understanding tone. "You have this multimillion—''

"Nothing controls me,'' he interrupted again. "Except what I feel for you and the boys. I used to think Starscape was my life, but it isn't. It's just my job. The five of you have become my life.'' No matter how he struggled, he couldn't keep the emotion out of his eyes. He let them bore into hers, so she could read his anger now.

"That isn't true of you, however, is it? You love the boys but I'm just the playboy uncle you'll make love with, but don't consider worthy of a place in your life. Come on, buckle up. The boys will be waiting for us.''

"I accepted your proposal, didn't I?'' she demanded, angry now, as well as confused.

"Yeah, but apparently only because the sex was good."

She backhanded him in the chest. "That's a rotten thing to say!"

"But not as bad a suggestion that being a full-time father might get on my nerves."

"Why are you making such a big deal out of that?" she demanded. "Every guy in the Daddy Club admits to that."

"But they're still there." He turned the key in the ignition.

"My point exactly. We're arguing on the same side."

"No, we're not." He drove to the exit and waited for an opening in the traffic. "If we were on the same side you'd have signed the contract."

THEY STARED SILENTLY at the road all the way home. Susan had never felt more miserable.

She was temporarily distracted from the gloom surrounding her when the boys welcomed her with genuine delight. Then they crowded around, freshly bathed and in their pajamas, to see what she'd brought them. Burgie leaped on Aaron, then on Susan, his bushy tail wagging. Then he sat beside the boys like a fifth child.

Ringo, she noticed, was on his feet and insisting on his place in the group.

Susan pulled out four long-sleeved T-shirts and distributed them. Ringo fought her when she tried to help him put his on, until his head got caught in the sleeve.

"Dad-dy!" he wailed clearly.

Aaron came to his rescue without looking her way.

She presented the boys with coin banks in the shape of the Statue of Liberty, and Yankee baseball caps.

John rattled his bank. Coins clinked inside.

"Those are from Paulette and Micah," Susan said.

Paul examined the bottom, trying to figure out how to retrieve the coins.

"It's to save," Aaron said, righting it and handing it back to him, "not to spend. If you guys cleaned your rooms and helped Beebee with the dishes, you'll have your allowance to spend on Saturday."

The housekeeper appeared behind them. "They were a big help to me," she said. "John took out the garbage, Paul set the table, and George helped clear it. Ringo kept Burgie out of our way."

Susan handed her a T-shirt and a baseball hat.

"Thank you," she said pulling the shirt on over the housedress she always wore. Then she put the hat on and did a turn for the boys. "How do I look?"

"Great," John said. "But it doesn't matter how you look. Can you play?"

She raised a superior eyebrow. "I can pitch fast-balls, knuckleballs, sliders and change-ups. I could even send spitballs, but they won't let me."

John blinked in surprise and turned to Aaron. "Can she really?"

He nodded. "She's won the last three Starscape games for us against Microsoft."

"Wow!"

"And I thought you couldn't play because you were—" John stopped himself, no doubt sensing he was on dangerous ground.

"A woman?" Beebee asked, pretending to think

about it. "No, that can't be it, because I've seen Susan play with you and you treat her like a teammate. Is it because I'm old maybe?"

John winced. "Not old but, you know, not really young."

Beebee took his honesty with good grace and gave him a hug. "I'm young in my heart, John, and that keeps my body going. You shouldn't decide someone isn't good at something just because you don't *think* they would be."

"Amen," Aaron said, giving the word a subtle emphasis that wasn't lost on Susan. "Burgie been out lately?"

"Not since before dinner," Beebee replied.

At the word "out," Burgie began to leap about excitedly. Aaron took him into the backyard.

Susan walked the boys up to bed, tucked them in, then came back down for a much-needed cup of tea. Beebee was already at work on it, dunking a little egg-shaped infuser into a steaming mug. The aromatic bergamot in the blend filled the kitchen.

"Is it my imagination," Beebee asked, putting the infuser aside and handing Susan the mug, "or are you and Aaron not speaking to each other?"

Susan sat at the table. "As usual, Bee, you see all."

"Your boss wouldn't let you move the show to Seattle?"

Susan explained what had happened, including Aaron's offer to leave the business in care of his second-in-command.

Beebee looked puzzled. "That's good, isn't it?"

"So it would seem. But I suggested that, instead of Aaron giving up everything, maybe I should just turn down the offer and we'll all go to Seattle with him. That's what set him off.''

"But I thought you felt the boys should stay here.''

Beebee's eyes were unsettlingly watchful. Susan blew into her tea to avoid them. "Maybe I was wrong.'' She glanced up to catch the housekeeper's speculative gaze, then Aaron walked in with Burgie, and Beebee pushed away from the table.

"I'm off to bed,'' she announced pushing in her chair. "Unless there's something in the laundry you brought back that can't wait until tomorrow?''

"Nothing, Beebee. Go on to bed.''

"All right. Glad to have you both back safe and sound. There's decaf in the pot, Aaron.''

"Thanks, Bee.''

IN NO MOOD TO BE conciliatory, Aaron poured a cup of coffee, said a polite if stiff good-night to Susan and went into the family room with Burgie and the Sunday paper.

Apparently she shared his attitude because a moment later the downstairs light went out and he heard her footsteps on the stairs.

He had no idea what to do about her. He felt as though his body had been buried in sand up to his neck and he was unable to move in any direction. He didn't think he could live without her and the boys, but she was making it damned difficult.

He opened the sports page, but instead of reading, he went over in his mind the afternoon's argument. Still, he could make no sense of it.

He'd insisted that she sign the contract that would make her a household name; he'd promised to care for the children so that she could fulfill her obligations—but she'd resisted.

Then she'd offered to give it all up and follow him to Seattle with the boys and he'd refused her.

What was wrong with them?

Less than a month ago he'd been convinced that Starscape defined him, but now he was willing to give it up for a while. And Susan had insisted that she couldn't love a man devoted to his work, but last Friday she'd agreed to marry him.

Why wasn't that progress? Why were they still as far apart as they'd been the day they met?

He hadn't a clue.

Too tired to try to figure it out he folded the paper and tried to concentrate on the news from the Mariners' spring training camp.

But a scream that raised the hair on the back of his neck came from upstairs. It was shrill and long and female.

He took the stairs three at a time, Burgie still outdistancing him, and found the three older boys and Beebee collected at the foot of Susan's bed. Burgie went to the blankets bunched at the foot and whined.

Susan stood in her nightshirt on her pillows, leaning back against the brass headboard, her face contorted in an expression of terror mingled with disgust.

Aaron came around the bed to her. "What is it?" he asked.

She edged toward him, pointing to the rumpled bedcover at the foot. "Something in there crawled over me," she said, her voice trembling. "It was cool and slimy."

A shudder accompanied that last word. He grasped her by the waist and lifted her off the bed.

"Uh-oh," John said.

Paul and George both took a step backward.

"What?" Aaron asked, thinking that he'd come to dread that word.

John shifted his weight. "Well," he said with a nervous glance at his brothers, "it...it could be Frank."

"Who's Frank?" Susan asked, placing her body strategically behind Aaron's.

"Well...we were putting him in the tub when you came home, and we ran downstairs and forgot all about him. And he can...you know...jump."

As John said this, Frank chose that moment to prove what he was capable of. He leaped a good foot off the rumpled blankets with a deep definitive, "Rib-bet!"

Susan shrieked.

The frog landed on the carpet on the far side of the bed and disappeared under the desk.

The boys went fearlessly in pursuit. They emerged moments later with the slimy bug-eyed creature, his long legs dangling.

"Do we got to let him go?" George asked plain-tively.

Aaron turned to Susan.

Still pale and peering out from behind his shoulder, she swallowed. "You can keep him on the service porch."

George grinned broadly. "Thanks, Mom!" he said. The boys ran downstairs in a parade to do just that.

Beebee rolled her eyes. "I'd better go supervise.

Just what we need—one more mouth to feed. Do you think he likes his flies grilled or sautéed?''

"Good night," Aaron said.

Beebee peered around him to look at Susan. "Do you want me to bring you up a brandy or something?''

Susan shook her head, her arms folded tightly. Her dark hair tumbled about her slender shoulders in appealing disarray.

Aaron shoved his hand in his pockets. "Everything all right now?''

She looked in dismay at the damp clump of sheets and blanket. "Yes, thank you. I'll be fine.''

"You never did get that extra set of bedding did you?" he asked.

"No, but that's okay. I'll just pull off the sheets and sleep on the mattress pad.''

IF SUSAN EXPECTED a chivalrous offer to share his bed, she was sadly mistaken. He pulled the offending sheets off her bed and said coolly, "Sleep well. I'll put these in the laundry room. See you in the morning.''

Susan checked on Ringo, found him still fast asleep but uncovered as usual. She pulled up his blankets, then returned to her room to lie on the bare mattress pad under a blanket. She stared at the ceiling, wondering where it had all gone wrong.

She couldn't understand his attitude. Why was he offended by her offer to move to Seattle? When they'd first admitted to feelings for each other, he'd as much as said that was the only way it could work between them.

And now that she'd grown enough that she could think about giving up her show and the astounding offer to make their life together work, he was hurt?

That didn't make sense—unless he'd grown, too.

She tried to follow that thought to some reasonable explanation for the current state of their relationship, but the warrens of her mind were too cluttered with confusion, and reason escaped her.

She heard Aaron bring the boys back upstairs and into their rooms, his deep voice quietly bidding them a final good-night.

"Good night, Dad!" the boys chorused from their rooms.

Susan put her pillow over her head and tried to sleep.

Chapter Thirteen

Susan awoke determined to make things right.

She remembered Aaron's predawn drive to convince her that she should accept the company's offer, and his promise to stay and help with the boys.

How could she have thrown that back in his face?

Some need to gain the upper hand in their relationship by being the one who gave the most, perhaps? She wasn't sure. Whatever it was, she'd done it unconsciously, and now that she'd had time to think about it, she knew she was wrong.

She got the children down to breakfast, took a phone call for Aaron while he was in the shower, found shoes, homework, John's backpack. Paul, still on suspension, would go to day care with George and Ringo so that she could talk to Aaron.

She would send Beebee shopping.

She met him at the French doors when he came in with Burgie after the dog's morning comfort stop.

"Do you have plans for this morning?" she asked, smiling into his neutral expression.

The neutrality became suspicion. "No. I figured I'd watch the boys while you get ready for tomorrow night's talk. You do remember you're expected at Hardware and Muffins?''

''Thanks. I did forget.'' But it didn't matter. Her dealer had called with a fireplace just before she'd left for New York. She could pick it up and plan the installation for tomorrow's session.

She met Aaron's gaze, ''I'm sending the boys to day care so you and I can talk.''

He did not look receptive. ''If it's going to be more of what you had to say yesterday, I don't think I want to hear it.''

''I was wrong,'' she put in quickly. ''Do you want to hear that?''

He studied her a moment without a change of expression, then drew a breath and nodded. ''Okay, that's a start.''

''Good,'' she said. ''I'll take the boys to day care. drop Beebee at Ruth Naomi's—they're going shopping—then I'll bring home a couple of her muffins and we'll talk.''

''All right.'' His expression softened. ''But I'll drive the boys and Beebee.''

''No, you have to return a phone call.'' She handed him the message she'd taken for him. ''From Ted. He called while you were showering. He said to call him after you've had breakfast.''

He tucked it in the pocket of his flannel shirt. ''Thank you.''

She looked into his still serious expression and thought she found a glimmer of lust in it. ''Can you be more grateful than that?'' she asked.

''After the night I've had,'' he warned dryly, ''don't mess with me.''

She framed his face in her hands, brought it down within reach of her lips and kissed him for all she was worth. She felt the ice thaw in him and the anger evaporate.

"Hold that thought," she said, "until I get back from town."

"You got it," he promised.

SHE RETURNED HOME with two caramel-peach muffins, a speeding ticket and a heart filled with hope.

Aaron, on the cordless phone, was facing the kitchen window while he made notes on a message pad.

She kissed his upper arm and began to brew a fresh pot of coffee.

Her quick stop at Hardware and Muffins got her thinking about what she could do for that particular audience that would last an entire season of five shows a week.

Jekel had suggested a complete remodel. Maybe she should rethink the fireplace as tomorrow's class and plan it into a segment. Ruth Naomi might be disappointed, but once she explained that Jekel wanted to use her store, she'd be thrilled.

And once she heard about the Daddy Club's involvement, she'd be delirious with joy.

Susan was pulling down a pair of mugs when she heard Aaron say, "So Barb got me a flight out tonight?"

She lost control of the mugs, and one fell into the sink and shattered.

Aaron turned at the sound, his expression grim.

Her good cheer fell in on itself. When she'd first

heard him mention the flight, she'd thought it had
something to do with the new product launch. But
she could tell by his face that it didn't. Something
was wrong at Starscape.

"Okay, thanks, Ted. I'll just go straight to the office if you're going to be there. Right. Bye."

Susan put down the surviving mug and asked
calmly, "You have to go home?"

Aaron placed the phone back on its countertop
stand and looked into her eyes. "Yes I do. A takeover
bid we'd thought we averted seems to be coming at
us again. I have a good crew, but this is something I
have to take care of."

It was only a moment before the old bitterness
forced itself forward, but she bit it back, reminding
herself of what she'd learned since then.

"How long will you be gone?" she asked.

"I'm not sure. It depends on how stubborn they
are. It could be over in a week or it could take a
month or more."

"So." A month. Or more. It was hard to be understanding and philosophical. She'd known this
would happen. And she hated being right.

She poured coffee into the cup, her hand trembling
against her struggle to remain calm. "You thought I
was being foolish when I didn't sign the contract."
She put a splash of cream into the coffee and handed
the mug to him.

He took it from her and put it down on the counter.
"The fact that I have to leave," he said quietly,
"doesn't mean that I want to. Or that I won't hurry
back as quickly as I can. I can see what's going on

in your head, Susan. I thought we had this out. I thought you'd reconsidered and understood.''

"I do understand," she said wearily. "You don't choose to go, you have to go. But that doesn't change the reality. It was a good thing I didn't sign the contract, because whether you mean to or not, you're leaving the boys. And one of us should be with them."

He closed his eyes, obviously summoning patience. "Susan, this is no ordinary problem that anyone can handle. This is about ownership of the company and right now I hold it. I *can* live without it. It *isn't* who I am anymore. But I built it with everything I had inside me and with everything my friends and co-workers gave me to make it work. And I'll be damned if I'll let that fall uncontested into someone else's hands. This isn't just another bridge in Central America."

She couldn't think clearly. She couldn't reason. All she knew was that she'd been right all along. This wasn't going to work.

"I understand that." She smiled thinly. "I know you care—about everyone—but you've put back a spark in the boys' lives that your business is going to force them to live without too often." She sighed, feeling the tearing in two of all her dreams for them. "I think the best thing for us to do is to go on as we thought we would originally. I'll give them a home, and you come for Christmas—or whenever you can."

AARON FOUND HER CALM almost harder to bear than her ranting would have been. It was as though her passion was gone because she felt sure there was no longer a reason for it.

"Susan, I won't let you write me off," he said, taking hold of her arms. "I have to go, but I'm coming back."

"I know," she said. "Then you'll have to leave again for one reason or another. I understand that a business that size doesn't run itself. This all probably happened in the first place because you've been away. We have to accept what is."

He looked heavenward in supplication and gave her a shake. "We don't have to *accept* anything. You say you understand, but you're pushing me out because this reminds you of your past, and you don't want to deal with it again."

"The boys—"

"Need me. I know that. And I need them. I know Becky and Dave gave you custody, so legally the boys are yours. But the kids have given themselves to me in a way the courts could never affect. They're not going to let you close the door on me."

She looked as though something was bleeding inside her. He shook her again, trying to refocus her attention on him rather than on her pain.

"While I'm gone," he said, "I want you to sign that contract and return it by courier. Beebee will help you with the boys until I get back."

"No," she said firmly.

He dropped his hands, hope waning that he could turn this around. "Then you don't trust me, after all."

"I don't trust you to be able to affect a force that's grown bigger than you are. It's no longer something you control." She pulled the ring off her finger and tried to hand it to him. "Here. You should take this back."

He held his hands stiffly at his sides, but every retort he could think of involved foul words or raising his voice several decibels. He turned away, instead, grabbed his jacket and walked out the door.

He walked for miles, bought a Polish dog from a vendor at a strip mall, then walked from shop to shop just to work off his misery. He rode home in a cab, arriving just as Susan was returning with the boys from school and day care.

Susan eyed his large packages and gave him a look that told him presents would not diminish the boys' loneliness in his absence.

"Come on, guys," he said as they crowded around him. "Let's go upstairs and check out these boxes. We have to talk about something."

The boys led the way, excitement and greed making them loud and rambunctious as they all crowded into John's and Paul's room.

Aaron put the packages on the bed, handed one to each of the older boys, then sat on the bed with Ringo in his lap and helped him open his.

John ripped open his box and stared in surprise at the contents, then looked at Aaron. "I don't get it. Is it…cookies?"

Aaron nodded, pulling the tall clear container out of Ringo's box. Ringo scrambled off Aaron's lap, took the plastic cylinder and held it in both arms, then marched around the room declaring "Mine! Mine!"

Aaron took John's container to illustrate his point as the other boys crowded around him. Ringo pushed his way in.

"There are thirty cookies in here," he said. "And I'm giving them to you because my business in Seattle is having a problem, and I have to be gone for what's probably going to seem like a long time."

The older boys' faces fell.

"I know," he said quickly. "I don't like it, either. But I have to go. This puts my friends in trouble, too, and I have to go to Seattle and make sure they keep their jobs and lots of other things that are important to them."

"How long?" John asked.

"I won't let it be more than thirty days," Aaron said.

John and Paul made faces at each other.

George didn't understand, but apparently presumed by his brothers' expressions that it couldn't be good.

Ringo climbed back into his lap.

"That's three times ten," John said, "five times six, and four times...um...well, it's a lot!"

Aaron nodded. "I know. It's a lot for me, too. But what I want you to do every day, maybe when you come home from school—on weekends you can do it in the middle of the afternoon—have a cookie. Just one every day. Don't cheat, okay? Just one. And by the time you're done with the cookies, I'll be home."

Paul, ever resourceful, suggested brightly, "Why don't we just come with you?"

Aaron stroked his hair. "Susan can't come because she has to do her show, so you guys have to stay and take care of her for me."

George looked worried. "You're gonna go in a plane."

He drew him closer. "Yes, I am. But you know

what? I can call you on my cell phone from the plane to let you know I'm fine. That'll be just about the time you guys are climbing into bed. And then I'll call you in the morning to let you know I got there.''

"You promise you won't crash?" Paul asked.

John elbowed his brother. "Don't be stupid. God makes planes crash. He's not the boss of God. Nobody is."

Aaron drew them all closer. "I can't say absolutely, but I'm pretty sure I won't crash. And by the time you're finished with your cookies—maybe even before—I'll be back. And here. I got you some shirts, too.''

The boys were more interested in the cookies. "Do we get one today?" George wanted to know.

John shook his head. "We don't get to have one till he's gone. So we start tomorrow, right?"

"Right."

Susan offered to drive Aaron to the airport just to show him she could do it. But he told her Ted had arranged for a car to pick him up.

When she answered a knock at the door and came face-to-face with a liveried driver, she experienced a weird sense of déjà vu.

She remembered standing on the church steps and watching Aaron arrive in a limo. She'd had no idea then how completely he would affect her life and the boys'.

She'd written him off as a playboy whose family came second to his work. Now she understood that he didn't choose to put his family second; it just happened because of the nature of his work.

Aaron came down the stairs carrying Ringo, the boys trailing him with long faces. He kissed Ringo, then handed him to Beebee, whom he wrapped in a hug.

"Take care," she said, her voice thick. "And don't worry about anything. I'm in charge, you know."

"I know." He hugged each of the other boys in turn, then scratched the dog's neck.

"How many cookies a day?" he asked the boys.

"One!" they shouted in unison.

"Very good. I love you. Take care of Susan and Beebee."

"We will," John promised, his voice high. George and Paul began to cry.

Aaron caught Susan's arm and pulled her with him onto the porch. The night was dark, the driver standing a discreet distance away. Aaron took her in his arms and kissed her soundly as though he were branding her.

"Watch for me," he said in her ear. "I'll be back."

Then he was gone, closed into the limo and disappearing down the road.

THE ATMOSPHERE AT DINNER was grim. The children picked at their food and no one spoke.

Susan tried to cheer them up by letting them leave their vegetables and have double desserts. Then she let them watch television a little longer before having their baths.

Susan went upstairs to help George. She pulled him out of the tub and wrapped him in a towel. When she went for his pajamas, she was surprised when he pulled on the bottoms but rejected the top.

"I want the shirt Daddy gave me," he said.

"What shirt?"

He led her into his room and showed her the shirt still lying in a nest of tissue. He held it up. It was a gray sweatshirt with the words My Dad Loves Me in bold letters. He handed her a smaller one. "This one's Ringo's."

She put it aside and helped George into his. "And tomorrow," he said, picking up a tall clear container filled with cookies, "I get to have one of these. And I can have one every day, and when Dad comes home they'll be all gone. Or maybe he'll come home before, we're not sure."

"I see." She noticed the same container near Ringo's crib, only his held baby biscuits.

"John and Paul gots 'em, too. Did you get one?"

Susan's throat constricted and a cold and lonely misery filled her. "Um...no, I don't think so. But I'm very glad you did."

She was not going to let herself succumb to missing him, she told herself firmly. This was precisely what she'd refused to live with ever again.

It wasn't his fault he had to go, but that didn't change the fact that he did.

The telephone rang and each boy scrambled to pick it up.

"Hi Dad!" they exclaimed from various parts of the house.

"He's in the plane!" George reported to her excitedly. He was perched on the edge of her bed. "And he's really high up! We didn't have to eat the carrots and we got two desserts, Daddy!"

He talked on for a few moments, then said "Okay.

I'll tell her. Tomorrow I'm gonna have a cookie. I know, just one. Okay. Love you, too. Bye, Daddy.''

Susan noticed as she tucked the boys in that the cheer factor had risen considerably. And each of the boys wore his special shirt. She managed to change Ringo into his without waking him.

Susan went downstairs to make her nightly cup of tea and saw Burgie lying dejectedly near Aaron's chair at the table. She got down on her knees to pet him and he rolled over shamelessly, feet curled, pleading for a rub.

"It's an odd thing," Beebee said, coming in with a stack of folded towels, "when a woman treats a dog better than she does a man."

Susan was not in the mood, but the woman had shown her and the boys nothing but kindness and support since she'd been here—even if it *was* mingled with enthusiastic interference.

"It's more complicated than it appears, Beebee," she said tactfully.

"Love is a pretty simple thing, really," the housekeeper replied, taking three dish towels off the top of the stack and putting them in a drawer. "You give it, and if you get it back with the same fervor, you don't count the cost."

"I tried to do that," Susan said in self-defense. The conversation distracted her for a moment from her attention to Burgie and he called her back by batting her with a thick paw. She resumed rubbing his chest and stomach. "I didn't sign my contract, because I *knew* something like this would happen and the boys would be left alone."

At Beebee's look of indignation, Susan raised a

placating hand. "I know you'd do everything you could and you're probably even better at it than I am, but the boys' parents left them to *me*. They're *my* responsibility. But I do love Aaron and I suggested it would be simpler if the boys and I just went to live in Seattle." She shrugged, still mystified by his refusal. "But he said no. Said I wanted to do that because I didn't trust him."

"And that's turned out to be true, hasn't it?" Beebee leaned a hip against the counter and rebuked her with a look. "No, he didn't whine to me. I forced it out of him while I helped him pack. He never had a mother who cared, so I've tried to be there for him. Which is a good thing, since you've apparently turned into a fair-weather friend."

Susan stood ready to do battle. "That isn't true Bee! I understand that he had to go, I just don't want to live that way again, and I don't see why I should have to! If he needs to be there, why is it so awful for me to need him to be here? Why is he more right than I am? I didn't force him into a choice, anyway."

"No, you just tried to give his ring back."

"We're not committed to the same things."

"I thought you were committed to each other. And to the boys."

Susan nodded. "So did I. But where is he?"

Beebee shook her head at her. "You know, the eighties and the nineties have produced some remarkable young women. I think it's wonderful that you'll tackle anything, that you're not afraid of anything, that you don't let anything stand between you and your dreams."

She picked up the stack of towels and stepped

closer to Susan. "But do you want to hear a simple truth? If you love anyone in this life—man, child, parent, whatever—it is not possible to have every single thing *you* want. If your family wasn't very strong, you might not understand this, but most families are like crossed lines that intersect but start and end in different directions.

"Everybody has a different point of view, a different goal in mind. And if you're going to remain part of it, your line's going to get crossed, smudged, maybe even some of it erased, because that's the reality of living with and loving other people."

"But I'm willing to give up my career to go with him!"

Beebee shook her head again, though her expression gentled. "That wasn't love, Susan, that was martyrdom. You wanted him to know how much loving him cost you."

Susan couldn't believe her ears.

"You love him by letting him be who he is—the boy who had the guts and the grace to make something huge and wonderful, when all he remembered was harassment and neglect. The man who'll let someone else care for that business for a year so you can have what you want."

"But the boys need at least one of us."

"They'll have you, even if they don't have you every single minute." She smiled apologetically. "I warned you when I first came here that I just barge in. But he's done so much for me, that I've pledged myself to do what I can for him. And I could tell when he called me to let me know he was staying in Princeton for a while that you were special, too.

You're a carpenter, remember? You can make things beautiful and, most important, you can make them *fit*.'' Beebee walked to the door, ''Good night, Susan.''

Susan checked on the boys before going to bed, pulled Ringo's covers up, then stopped in the middle of John's and Paul's room, her attention caught by their tall containers of cookies.

Her father had left her again and again all her life—but he'd never left her a container filled with cookies to count the days until he returned. And he'd never given her a sweatshirt that said he loved her.

She left the room in a hurry and waited until she was in her own before she burst into noisy sobs. When the storm abated somewhat, she sat on the edge of the bed wondering if she would ever be big enough to be able to live with a man who came and went all the time. Suddenly she noticed a foreign object on her desk. It was beige in color, sort of square...with a key pad?

She got up to investigate and discovered a fax machine.

A simple note taped to the front said, ''When it rings, push start.''

And as she stared at it in disbelief, it rang. It took her a moment to find the start key, but she did as ordered. A handwritten note began to inch its way out of the machine.

Hi, Susan—
Somewhere over Montana. When you wake the boys in the morning, please assure them I'm still alive. (I'd like to think you're not disappointed

about that.) Will call from the office first thing tomorrow. I left a business card under the apple magnet on the fridge. So call me if you need me. Or even if you don't.

—Aaron

Chapter Fourteen

The boys were down to seven cookies. John kept count.

Aaron e-mailed them every day, faxed cartoons and funny messages, and called several times a week. He never asked to speak to Susan. Of course, she never asked to speak to him, either.

She faxed him the children's school papers, pages out of their coloring books done especially for him, bawdy jokes Beebee had collected from Ruth Naomi.

But she never called him. She missed him abominably, which only reminded her that this could never work.

She'd called Jekel to explain her situation and tell him she wasn't signing the contract, after all. But he refused to accept that answer, told her they'd hold the offer open until the last possible moment. He called her every other day to see if she'd changed her mind.

The boys were a miracle.

John laughed and brought friends home all the time. Paul spent a lot of time on his computer, always calling her to come and see what he'd found on the encyclopaedia CD.

George was happy. He forced his way into the daily baseball games in the backyard by agreeing to chase the ball. He sent Aaron a page from his coloring book every single day.

Ringo seemed suddenly motorized. He ran everywhere, followed his older brothers, to their dismay, and had found an eager playmate in Burgie, who often went to the French doors and looked out, as though waiting for Aaron to appear.

Susan pushed Ringo in his baby swing one Saturday afternoon while the boys played baseball with their friends at the far end of the property. She watched the boys' new confidence, their developing dexterity, listened to the music of their laughter and realized she was doing all right as a mother.

She had a lot of help from Beebee, but the boys came to her for everything and shared eagerly with her. She loved that.

A foul ball fell some distance from them and rolled in their direction. George chased it and Susan headed toward it from her direction, hoping to save him a few steps. He'd been run ragged all afternoon.

She ruffled his hair and kissed his cheek. He would always stop for this attention, unlike his older brothers, who disdained such displays in front of their friends.

"They're running you all over the place," Susan sympathized.

"But they let me play!" he said, blind to any problem. "Dad says I'm gonna be a good runner when I grow up!"

"I know you are."

And then it hit Susan as though space debris had fallen out of the sky and landed on her head.

Aaron *was* here, even though he wasn't present physically. Everything he'd given the boys when he'd been home was strong enough to stay alive in them when he was gone.

And all his absentee input—e-mails, phone calls, faxes, the container of cookies, the shirts—were visible reminders of his love and concern.

That was what she'd missed in her childhood. Granted, not many people were e-mailing and faxing then—particularly not in Central America—but her father had seldom written and never called.

She stood still as the truth vibrated inside her. It wasn't that her father's absence had made her feel unloved. It was that she hadn't felt loved even when he was home.

In her child's mind she'd probably blamed it on his absences, but from this perspective, she could see that hadn't been the case at all.

But Aaron was with them, even when he wasn't.

"Mom?" George said.

She looked at him blankly.

"Mom!" John shouted from across the yard. "We need the ball!"

It was only then that she realized she still held it. She handed it to George and sent him on his way, aware belatedly that they'd called her Mom.

Behind her, Ringo shouted for another push.

But she stood still for a moment and let the smile form on her lips and fill her body. It bubbled up into a giggle, then burst into a laugh.

AARON, WITH TED AT HIS SIDE, sat across a board-room table from Whip Kimball of Kimdustries and his number-two man, Julian Rush, an earnest young fellow in wire-rim glasses. Aaron had learned over the past few days that both men were very smart and very determined.

But Aaron had been even more determined and Ted had been even smarter. A clever shuffle of stock and legal maneuvers kept them in control of Starscape. Aaron guessed that Ted's recent reconciliation with Sophia had put him at the top of his game.

Aaron refilled everyone's coffee from a carafe on the table and wondered at his own lack of emotion. He'd just saved his company from Kimdustries' aggressive bid to take over, and he was happy he'd saved jobs and careers for his staff and employees.

But he kept waiting for the elation he'd expected to feel for himself.

It didn't come.

He hadn't realized how right he'd been when he'd told Susan that Starscape no longer defined him. It was his baby, all right, but it was all grown-up now.

It didn't need him anymore. Or he didn't need it.

"Okay." Kimball leaned toward him, adding cream to his coffee, then handing the pitcher across the table to Aaron. "You're safe from me for now. But I'll only try again as soon as I find an opening."

Rush leaned toward Kimball and whispered something.

Kimball shifted in his chair and cleared his throat. "Julian and I were talking about this when we took a break this afternoon. Would you consider a merger?"

Aaron looked at Ted.

Ted shook his head. "Mergers are for sharing compatibilities, adding to a product line. We don't need what Kimdustries has."

Aaron turned to Kimball. "You have to admit he's right about that."

"You don't know everything about us," Kimball insisted. "Why don't we talk?"

Aaron glanced at the clock. It was after midnight, and he had a 4 a.m. date with a 747.

He pushed his chair back and got to his feet. "Why don't you call Ted about it next week?"

"Why can't we talk about it now?"

"Because I have a meeting on the East Coast." he offered each man his hand. "Good night."

Kimball got reluctantly to his feet and shook hands. "I'm looking forward to the next time," he said. "Goodbye, Bradley." He walked out the door, with Rush following.

Ted fell into his chair and took a long swallow of his coffee. "Why ask them to call *me* next week? We don't want to merge, do we?"

"I don't know. Do you?"

"No!"

"Then tell them that." Aaron gathered paperwork into his briefcase.

Ted poured more coffee. "Don't *you* have something to say about it?"

Aaron smiled at him as he zipped his case closed. "Not anymore. I'm selling you the company."

Ted spilled coffee all over himself and the table.

"I CAN'T BELIEVE THIS!" Ruth Naomi followed her around as Susan gathered up her tools. She'd just filmed the first of the many shows that would involve Hardware and Muffins. Jekel wanted this one done early to allow time to fine-tune any camera or production problems before moving into their every-day schedule.

They would also do the first segue into the weekly Daddy Club show. Neil Graber stood by, pale but calm, waiting for Susan to film the short walk across Hardware and Muffins to the Daddy Club's meeting place and announce its slot in the cable-network lineup.

"Do you know what you've done for us?" Ruth Naomi demanded. "Prepublicity alone has increased business twenty-one percent over the last two weeks!"

Susan paused in her work to hug her. "Do you have any idea what your friendship and Micah's and the Daddy Club has done for us?"

"Aren't we all so lucky? Isn't this the best thing that ever happened?"

On one level Susan had to agree. She couldn't imagine her life without the people who now filled it.

But on another level she wondered if her life would ever be right again. She'd faxed Aaron after her revelation yesterday, knowing that saving his company was probably keeping him too busy to take a call, but certain that once he received her plea to talk, he'd phone her.

But he hadn't. The boys had gotten e-mail, but there'd been nothing for her.

She could only conclude that he'd given up.

Guilt and regret nibbled at her insides, making her

feel desperate and alone, even while surrounded by Ruth Naomi, Paulette and the film crew, who were all good friends.

She felt as though some sophisticated software ran her body, because her heart was missing. It was somewhere in Seattle, looking for Aaron.

He'd be back eventually, she was sure, because he'd promised the boys. But it was becoming clear that he'd finally decided to believe her insistence that their relationship couldn't work. Just when she'd come to understand that it could.

The makeup girl touched up Susan's lipstick and gave the tip of her braid a quick brush.

"Is Beebee bringing the boys back here after the movie?" Ruth Naomi asked.

Susan straightened her overalls and tried to dredge up an on-camera attitude. "Yes, she is."

"Good. Because I'm taking us all out to dinner after the Daddy Club show to celebrate. Micah, Rose and Elaine and the kids, and the O'Gradys will meet us there."

Susan blinked at Ruth Naomi as Paulette cleared the area. "We'll take up the whole place!"

Ruth Naomi seemed pleased by that. "Power in numbers," she said. "I'd better get out of the way. Give them a great introduction."

Susan took her place in front of the camera, listened to the countdown and waited for the pointing finger that was her cue.

She began her spiel about the history of the Daddy Club and how *Susan's Workshop* had inadvertently launched this new addition to the Friday-night lineup.

She introduced Neil Graber, whose pallor had increased.

She told the audience about his work at Princeton University as she walked with him into an area set up with chairs opposite the coffee bar. The chairs were filled with many of the club's regulars.

"We might mention now," she said, "that you single dads out there are welcome to attend these meetings, and the number you'll see on your screen after the show is their hotline—you can call it any time of the day or night. That was set up for us by Darcie O'Grady, who turned one of the club's single dads into a married one.

"What's your topic tonight, Neil?"

He flashed a disarming smile at the camera. "Since I'm new at this and a little nervous, I've invited a panel of four fathers to talk about the problems special to dads with more than one child."

"I'm sure there's something there for all of us. I'll leave you to…"

Neil was supposed to announce his guest after Susan walked off-camera, but apparently forgetting that detail, he started early.

"I've invited Aaron Bradley, CEO of Starscape Software…"

Susan didn't hear the names of the others. Was Neil unaware that Aaron was out of town for…?

Before she could finish the thought, Aaron walked on camera with three other men and took his place in the lineup of chairs. All she could do was stare.

The camera followed Neil as he walked toward his guests, and Paulette had to yank Susan out of the way to prevent her from being run over.

When Paulette dragged her into the shadows behind the lights, Susan still drew in the sight of him,
trying to make sense of the situation.

Aaron *was* very much present, exuding a wit and
charm she knew the camera would love. He seemed
to have more input than the other fathers, and many
of the questions were directed at him. He replied with
calm, insightful and often funny answers.

Susan felt as though she'd stopped breathing.
Something was expanding in her chest, but it seemed
to be stealing her air rather than supplying it.

She couldn't tear her eyes from Aaron's dark blond
hair, burnished by the lights, his hazel eyes filled with
compassion and intelligence as he talked about the
children, his broad shoulders in a taupe silk shirt that
probably cost the earth. He wore brown slacks and
angled one leg on the knee of the other, clearly more
relaxed than the time he and Neil had blundered onto
her set.

Love, she thought, her brain beginning to work
again, relaxed you. It lit the dark, eased pain, dimin-
ished sorrow. It muted thunder.

Only, she'd been much later than Aaron in finding
that out. She wondered if he hadn't told her he was
coming home because he'd wanted to surprise her, or
because she'd worn down even *his* stubborn determination.

Twenty minutes into the show, Susan heard the
opening of a door followed by a stampede of feet and
the issuance of orders in a harsh whisper. "Stop!
Don't! You can't— Come here!"

She turned to look and was whirled completely

around as four little bodies ran past her, mindless of lights and cameras, and threw themselves at Aaron.

With an apologetic glance at the crew, Aaron opened his arms to his nephews, who in the past weeks had clearly become his sons.

"Is this where someone hollers 'Cut!'" Beebee asked dryly in Susan's ear. "I'm sorry. We were going to wait by the door, but John spotted Aaron on a monitor, pointed it out to his brothers, and I lost control of the situation."

Tears streamed down Susan's face. "It's okay," she said. "So have I."

AARON HAD NEVER SEEN anything more beautiful than the four boys running at him, pink-cheeked and bright-eyed and pushing each other out of the way to get to him. Though it would have been that much more beautiful if Susan had followed in their wake.

He'd done everything he could to make her want him home. His silence while he was gone had been calculated to prove that absence made the heart grow fonder. And his return without warning was supposed to catch her so off guard that she would listen to the love in her heart, rather than the concerns in her head, and admit that she needed and wanted him.

When a halt was called to the filming, Aaron hugged and kissed the boys, fussing over them as they tried to catch him up on three weeks' news in one minute.

"We have seven cookies left!"

"Burgie dragged Beebee through the hedge!"

"I got an A in math!"

"Susan cried 'cause you didn't answer her fax."

Susan cried?

Aaron looked over the boys' heads and saw Susan peering out of the shadows at him. He saw love and longing there—and tears. And in the flash of a light moved out of someone's way, he caught the wink of his ring on her finger.

He scooped up Ringo, caught George by the hand and told John and Paul to follow. Then he strode across the floor to her, the boys running to keep up.

"Dad's home!" John said excitedly when they reached Susan.

She swiped at her eyes. "I see that." She smiled up at Aaron. From across the floor he'd missed the uncertainty in her eyes, the confusion.

Well, he could clear that up in a hurry.

He noticed Beebee beside her for the first time and handed her Ringo. "Bee, please keep an eye on them for a few minutes so Susan and I can talk."

Beebee settled Ringo on her hip. "Glad to have you back." She grinned. "No one's ordered me around in weeks. Come on, guys. I think we can charm some treats out of Ruth Naomi."

"I want to stay with Dad!" George protested.

Aaron ruffled his hair. "Go with Beebee, then I'll show you all the cool things I brought you. I came straight from the airport, so I have it all with me."

"Can't we see it now?" Paul pleaded.

John smiled with superior knowledge. "They want to kiss or something. Come on. If we let them go now, they'll be back quicker and we'll get our stuff."

Beebee patted his head. "Child after my own heart." She winked at Aaron. "Don't forget to pick us up when you go home."

"Not a chance," he said. Then he caught Susan's hand, scanned the shop filled with camera crew, dads and the ever-watchful Ruth Naomi, and opted for a secluded corner between two high shelves of wall-paper-sample books.

He backed Susan into it, caught her chin in his hand and kissed her with all the pent-up need of the past three weeks.

He felt the rush of her response, the urgency in the arms wrapped around his neck, and the desperation betrayed by her right foot standing on his left.

Then she drew back and delivered a halfhearted punch to his chest. "Why didn't you call me back?" she demanded.

He frowned. "I didn't know you'd called me. Did you leave a message?"

"I faxed you."

"When?"

"Yesterday morning."

He nodded, understanding what had happened. "I'd been in a meeting for thirty-six hours. I told my secretary to let you or the children through if you called, but she mustn't have checked faxes. Then I went straight from the meeting to the airport."

She studied him skeptically, her eyes wide and brimming with tears and at last seemed willing to believe him. "Why didn't you tell us you were coming home?"

"Because I knew the boys would appreciate the surprise, and I wanted your unguarded response to seeing me." On the chance she hadn't noticed what that had been, he kissed his ring on her finger and reminded her. "You cried."

Her bottom lip quivered. "The boys…are happy to see you."

He kissed it. "And you aren't?"

She put her hands to his waist and leaned into him.

"Yes, I am. I missed you so much."

And hearing that was worth the few million he'd lost in making Ted an easy deal.

"What was in the fax?" he asked, pulling her closer. He could have sworn that he felt his soul re-unite with his body.

She dropped her forehead to his shoulder. "I told you that I'd come to realize that your love was with the boys and me all the time, even when you weren't. And that I felt sure that—" she raised her head and looked into his eyes, her own sincere and filled with love "—if it isn't too late, I think we'd make a wonderful family, wherever we are, even if you have to be away sometimes."

He kissed her for that, not just because it meant a lot to them as a family, but because she'd had to come to terms with her own past to reach that realisation—and it must have been hard.

"I have good news about that," he said finally, as her hands framed his face. "I sold Starscape to Ted. I'm now unemployed."

Her eyes widened in fascinated horror. "What?!"

"I sold Starscape, but don't worry. We can live extremely well and still send all the kids to an ivy league college."

"Aaron! You love your work!"

"I do, but I learned something, too, while I was gone. If I'm going to be a father, I should be here.

Many fathers don't have that choice and I sympathize with them, but I do. So I've made it.''

That time she kissed him, then looked at him with open adoration. His heart melted. "I could die for you right now," she whispered, "and do it with a smile on my face.''

"Don't even say that in jest," he scolded, "because I have big plans. I thought I'd stay with the boys while you work out your contract and see how you like filming five days a week. At the end of that time Ringo will be in school, and if you want to continue, fine. I might have a go at developing video games. Something challenging but nonviolent. Or, if you don't like it, maybe we can start some kind of business together. I have no idea what, but we have lots of time to plan.''

"How did you find time to think about all that," Susan asked, her heart swelling with love, "while you were saving your company from a takeover?''

"You and the boys were on my mind every minute of every day. That's why I knew it was time to get out.''

"You're absolutely sure about this?''

"Absolutely.''

"Even though I was so slow about understanding you?''

He grinned. "No problem. I still don't always understand *you*. But love doesn't seem to need that, does it?''

She hugged him with a squeal of delight. "I'll call the minister tomorrow. I wonder if there's ever been a wedding at Hardware and Muffins?''

If you enjoyed what you just read,
then we've got an offer you can't resist!

Take 2 bestselling
love stories FREE!
Plus get a FREE surprise gift!

Return to the charm of the Regency era with

GEORGETTE HEYER,

creator of the modern Regency genre.

Enjoy six romantic collector's editions with forewords
by some of today's bestselling romance authors,

Nora Roberts, Mary Jo Putney,
Jo Beverley, Mary Balogh,
Theresa Medeiros and Kasey Michaels.

Frederica
On sale February 2000

The Nonesuch
On sale March 2000

The Convenient Marriage
On sale April 2000

Cousin Kate
On sale May 2000

The Talisman Ring
On sale June 2000

The Corinthian
On sale July 2000

Available at your favorite retail outlet.

HARLEQUIN®
Makes any time special ™

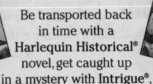

A special feeling,
   A special secret...
      No one blossoms more beautifully
         than a woman who's

With Child...

And the right man for her
will cherish the gift of love she brings.

Join American Romance and four
wonderful authors for the event of a lifetime!

THAT'S OUR BABY!
Pamela Browning
March 2000

HAVING THE BILLIONAIRE'S BABY
Ann Haven
April 2000

THAT NIGHT WE MADE BABY
Mary Anne Wilson
May 2000

MY LITTLE ONE
Linda Randall Wisdom
June 2000

Available at your favorite retail outlet.

HARLEQUIN®
Makes any time special ™

Visit us at www.romance.net

HARWC